Thrilling Thursday

A Tabitha Chase Days of the Week Mystery
(Book 2)

Denise Jaden

Denise Jaden Books

To Monica, one of my dedicated readers
who never fails to give me invaluable
feedback on early versions of my novels.
Thank you for everything. You make
the process of developing each mystery
much less stressful and a lot more fun!

Thrilling Thursday

A SEASIDE TOWN SELLING the supernatural, a fun-fair ride with a deadly twist, and a realtor-turned-sleuth rediscovering her purpose.

Tabby is settling into Crystal Cove, Oregon, and her new home on a magic-infused houseboat when the summer fair comes to town. She and her newly inherited cat, Sherlock, operate the coffee truck while screams of excitement erupt from nearby rides. Soon the fun screams turn to shrieks of horror when a dead body is discovered on one of the rides, and Tabby may be the only one who can help her detective friends figure out how it got there.

Apparently, Crystal Cove has no shortage of secrets or murders. Will Tabby's unique insight and gifting help her see through the town's shroud of illusions?

Join my mystery readers' newsletter today!

Sign up now, and you'll get access to a special mystery to accompany this series—an exclusive bonus for newsletter subscribers. In addition, you'll be the first to hear about new releases and sales, and receive special excerpts and behind-the-scenes bonuses.
Visit the link below to sign up and receive your bonus mystery:

https://www.subscribepage.com/mysterysignup

Chapter One

When my Aunt Lizzie told me about the magic of Crystal Cove, I'd always thought she meant magic that involved witches, warlocks, and fortune-telling. I'd lived here for almost three months, and okay, Crystal Cove did boast its fair share of witches and fortune-tellers (although I'd yet to meet a warlock), but the real magic, I'd come to believe, was in the sense of belonging this seaside town brought me.

I looked around at the bright twinkling lights on the rides at the summer fair and let out a happy sigh. This fair took the town's magic to a whole new level.

"Excuse me? How long will that take? Fair's gonna open soon."

I blinked and shook my head to bring myself back to the present. I looked from the espresso machine on the coffee truck down to the two carnival employees waiting for their drinks. "Just another sec. That was two double espressos, right?"

A third guy had appeared behind them while I was lost in thought. "Make it three." He had a stripe of blue hair down one side of his otherwise blond head.

"Need something to keep us awake in this sleepy town," the impatient guy in the red baseball cap said.

Funny how others could see the same town in completely different ways. But I could grasp his reasoning. These carnies traveled around from big cities to tiny towns, setting up their rides and booths, and in comparison to other bustling cities, Crystal Cove probably didn't appear to hold much interest to these guys barely into their twenties. I'd grown up in Portland, and the idea of being a nameless face lost in a crowd was what had lost its sheen.

I passed them their coffees and offered a bright smile. "On the house."

I waved away red baseball cap's ten-dollar bill. He squinted at me, not immediately pulling the bill away. Even though he wore the same type of distressed jeans and black T-shirt as his friends, his didn't look as dirty. I could tell by his wary gaze that people didn't comp these guys often. Still, I couldn't help myself. I wanted to paint Crystal Cove in a better light for all of them. Eventually, he stuffed his money away.

"Thanks!" the guy with the blue striped hair said with exuberance, while the third guy had already turned away, seemingly oblivious to the nicety.

As they left with their espressos, I pulled my own ten-dollar bill out of my purse and fed it into the till. The café owner, Olivia, had been on me about giving away free coffees and bakery items at the café, and I had the sense she'd feel no more generous with her coffee truck. She was a nice lady, but she reminded me again and again that she was running a business.

I probably should have had more understanding, having started up my own business recently. Frank, the local marina owner, had put me in touch with a few owners who wanted to rent out their houseboats. Even though my skill set lay more in selling real estate, I'd spent the last few months learning all about property management and was getting the hang of it. Still, I was a lot less business-minded than the family I'd come from, and what was the big deal if I bought people coffee once in a while?

Except that if I did it as often as I liked, I'd be broke in no time. As two of the carnies headed toward their respective booths in the food section of the fair, and the blue-haired guy angled toward the midway, I felt my phone vibrate in my pocket. I pulled it out to see a new text from Rachael.

~Sorry! Running late! The renters arrived early, so I'm letting them in and getting them set up. Can you watch my booth until I get there?~

I stared over at the art booth I'd set up in the tiny crafts section of the fair, between the snacks and the midway. It was probably only thirty feet away, but still, I didn't know quite how I'd manage both the art booth and the coffee truck if either had a sudden influx of customers.

But our deal had been that if Rachael cleaned the houseboats I managed, I would set up her booth. The renters weren't supposed to arrive until the next morning, but if she didn't show them around, I'd have to leave to do it, so what choice did I have?

~Sure~ I texted back. ~But hurry if you can.~

I'd barely finished typing when the local businessman who had brought in the fair, Mr. Klaus, called out over a bullhorn, "Crystal Cove Summer Fair is open for business!" He unhooked the large rope that separated the fairgrounds from the parking lot, and a hoard of excited patrons rushed through.

I glanced at Rachael's art booth. I'd convinced her to book space at the fair in the first place. Word Art, as she called her booth, included canvases with elaborate single words or phrases, decorated to enhance their theme. I'd already paid her to repaint the Lady of Fortune moniker on my late aunt's houseboat, as well as commissioned a piece with the name of my newly inherited cat, Sherlock. It had ended up being a telling piece—with whiskers on the S, a low-lying belly in the middle of the word, and haphazard blue jewels decorating the letters.

As customers split off between the food section, the craft section, the midway, and the rides, a wash of guilt came over me. I couldn't leave Rachael's booth unattended when she'd worked so hard on every single canvas.

I scribbled a "BACK IN 5 MINUTES" sign for the coffee truck, locked up the till, and rushed across to Rachael's booth, just as the first customers arrived.

"That's so cool!" a girl of about twelve told her mom. "Can I get my name done?"

The mother turned to me. "How much to paint the name Liana?"

Rachael had just started adding names to her collection of art. The problem was, she wasn't here to paint originals right now.

"If you could come back in about half an hour, the artist should be here. She can give you prices on original pieces, if that's what you're looking for."

The mother nodded and seemed to make a promise to her daughter as they strode off together.

More customers arrived and liked what Rachael already had on display. Many were even interested in purchasing, but they all decided they didn't want to carry the canvases around with them, and they'd come back at the end of the night.

The coffee shop had formed a lineup by this time, people glancing around for the barista. I was surprised at how busy all of the food vendors were already. It was seven o'clock on a Thursday, the first night of the fair. I would have expected most patrons to have just had dinner and raced toward the rides.

I'd had Rachael's artwork prominently displayed on the table at the front of her booth, but I started moving it to behind the table so I could race over and catch up on coffee orders. I was just scrawling the same kind of "BACK IN 5 MINUTES" sign for Rachael's booth when Mr. Klaus interrupted me.

"What's with no one manning the coffee truck? I did Olivia a favor by saving a spot for her, and now you're not even there?" Mr. Klaus was a wiry guy with angular features that made him look perpetually angry. Or maybe he just was perpetually angry.

"I'm headed right back there now!" I told him, racing out from behind Rachael's booth.

"People are complaining. And now who's going to watch this art booth?" He shook his head. "And here I thought Miss

Adams was serious when she said she'd be a responsible vendor."

Everyone in town had fought for booth space when Mr. Klaus posted a note in the local paper that he was limiting local vendors this year. Apparently, he'd had to allow the carnival to bring in several of their own vendors in order to book them at the last minute. The fairgrounds really were packed from one end to another.

Rachael had been charming when she went into his mini golf establishment to apply for a spot in person. I suggested she make up a piece of word art just for him. She'd found out his first name and had made up a manly decorative piece with "Bryan Klaus" at the center of the canvas. A week later, she'd received an email that he had reserved a small booth space for her art, as long as there was no woo-woo magic involved, and he'd take forty percent of her profits, which I thought was steep, but she had agreed.

Of course forty percent of nothing was nothing, and Mr. Klaus knew that. He had allowed a local candle crafter a booth, as well as a honey supplier and a local clown who made balloon animals, but that was pretty much it for locals, so both Rachael and Olivia knew how fortunate they had been to get their own space at the fair.

I opened my mouth to try and come up with an excuse, but before I could, I saw Rachael racing through the entry to the fairgrounds, her black minidress showing off her black-and-white striped tights.

"She's here now!" I practically yelled as I made my way past Mr. Klaus and toward the line of patrons at the coffee truck. I waved Rachael toward her art booth.

Thankfully, Mr. Klaus was concerned enough about making a profit that he didn't stop me, but he looked Rachael up and down and muttered, "What is she wearing?" as I left.

For a man who lived in a town that made a living from passing-through tourists who were here for the supernatural, Bryan Klaus was surprisingly opposed to anything otherworldly. Rachael knew it, too, and had purposely played down her magic aspirations and played up her artistic ability when she approached him for booth space. I was certain she had intended to change out of her black-and-white striped tights before arriving at her booth tonight, but she must not have had time.

I tried not to feel too bad about this as I concentrated on catching up on the line of coffee customers. I'd been working at the café for three months and was getting better at pouring foamy milk with one hand and sprinkling decorative flavors on top with the other. As I finally finished with the last order, my phone rang in my pocket. I pulled it out and saw it was my mom. She called to check in when my dad wasn't around. He hadn't forgiven me for ditching my life in Portland and making a sudden move to Crystal Cove, but I thought my mom was secretly happy that I'd chosen to take care of her sister's boat, rather than selling it. I clicked my phone onto speakerphone as I cleaned up from the rush.

"Hi, honey. Everything okay with you?" It was how she started every conversation. With the sudden and unexpected suicide of her sister, she could never relax until I assured her I was fine.

"I'm good, Mom. We have a summer fair going on in Crystal Cove, and Olivia has me running the coffee truck." I'd learned that if I gave honest specifics, she calmed down a lot faster than if I kept it vague.

"Oooh, that sounds like fun. Listen, honey, would you call and check in with Pepper when you have a chance? She's not returning my calls and I'm worried."

My sister, Pepper, was in her second year of medical school. I had no doubt she was simply swamped with coursework, and with Mom's sensitivity, she may have been waiting less than a day to hear back from her youngest daughter.

Regardless, I knew what I had to say. "For sure, Mom. I'll call her as soon as I have a chance, but I'm sure she's just busy with school." I turned to clean the rear counter and brought my phone with me.

"And you're still planning a trip here next month for your high school reunion, right?"

This topic was trickier. My ten-year high school reunion was coming up in Portland, and whenever Mom pushed me for a date of when I might come home for a visit, I'd offered this as a possible suggestion. But the closer my reunion loomed, the more I didn't want to go. My high school friends had always been the type who thrived on one-upping one another. I couldn't even imagine what Molly Tinsdale would say about my big accomplishment of becoming a barista in a small seaside town. Moving to Crystal Cove had given me a new outlook on what good friendships could feel like. But besides that, I didn't look forward to staying in my parents' house when my father wasn't even speaking to me.

"The houseboat rental market is starting to heat up, Mom. I won't know until closer to time." I closed my eyes through my mom's sigh. I knew she was lonely, with all three of her kids now out of reach and my dad, the senator, working eighty hours a week. I couldn't solve all of her problems, though. I had barely started to get a handle on mine.

"Well, let me know as soon as you know," she said, as though admitting defeat. "I think you'd have fun at your reunion." She'd barely finished talking when a throat cleared behind me.

"Oh, listen, Mom, I have to run, but I'll call you later, okay?"

After saying goodbye and hanging up, I stared down at my phone for several seconds, knowing I should call Pepper right away so I didn't forget. But then another cleared throat reminded me why I couldn't.

As I turned, trying to reset my mind from my phone call to my job, my eyes widened. I knew my next customer.

"Fancy meeting you here," he said with a wink.

Detective Jay Jameson was a new friend in town. He had helped clear my name in a murder investigation when I first arrived in Crystal Cove and I appreciated him for it. He was also probably the best-looking man I'd ever set eyes on in real life, but I was doing my best to play it cool and not let on that I thought so. I'd decided soon after arriving that while I tried to get my life in order, I had to put all thoughts of dating anyone, even someone this attractive, out of my mind.

"High school reunion, huh? I love going to those things, even if they're not mine." Jay was around thirty, a couple of years older than me, so I imagined his own high school reunion had come and gone. "It's a rush to get people together ten years later, look at photos, and see how everyone has changed."

My cheeks warmed, as though he'd be able to see every ounce of my insecurity about it. I waved a casual hand. "I probably can't even go. My mom just wants me to visit and was hoping that weekend might work."

He must have heard the unease in my voice because he looked over my side menu board and changed the subject. "I heard you might be manning the coffee truck tonight. What do you recommend?"

So far, I hadn't gotten a clear handle of how Jay preferred his coffee—strong and bitter or sweet and decorative. Every time he came to the café, he made me choose what to make him, and all he ever said in response was, "It's pretty good."

I sighed. "Let me guess. You're not even going to give me a hint at your favorite so far?"

He smirked, highlighting one of his dimples.

I'd been learning new coffee recipes over the past three months. Part of the charm of The Heirloom Café, where I usually worked in the evenings, was that we always offered unique specials. When Olivia hired me, she told me she'd be counting on me to come up with some original coffee recipes, so I'd been working hard at it.

"Fine. Okay. I have just the thing." I didn't know if that was true, but I hoped my forced confidence might rub off on him. For the summer fair, I'd come up with two coffee truck specials. One was a brown sugar Irish coffee, and the other was a coconutty iced latte. I whipped up the brown sugar Irish coffee for him, and after adding the Irish whiskey-flavored heavy whipped cream I'd blended earlier, I sprinkled on some sweet coconut flakes. It was a combination of the two specials. I liked making him something unique and not giving him the same recipe I served everyone else.

I held out the drink, and he passed me a twenty. We'd had plenty of arguments about him overpaying. I always wanted to treat, but he'd finally worn me down and made me take his money. I took it now and made his change, but he dropped all of it into my tip jar, more than paying for the three carnies I'd treated earlier.

I rolled my eyes, mostly to cover up any blush to my cheeks. "Twenty dollars for a coffee? That seems worth it," I said sarcastically.

He shrugged. "It is. Now when can I take you on the Ferris wheel?"

"I'm more interested in the bumper cars," I told him, "or that wavy ride that goes in circles really fast."

"We can try those, too. When do you get a break?"

I nibbled my lip and glanced in Rachael's direction. That was when I saw my cat, Sherlock, at her feet. How had he gotten here? Had she brought him from my boat?

She was busy painting on a canvas for a couple at her booth. Rachael had a terrible crush on Detective Jameson. He knew it and had hinted to me that she was too young for him. Which she was. But she was my friend and I still couldn't fathom walking around the fair and going on rides with Jay when it would definitely make her jealous.

At the same time, I was trying to make new friends in this town, not snub them.

"Olivia might be by later," I hedged. She had promised to come and give me a break after she closed the café for the night. "But if it's busy, the truck might take two of us."

Jay nodded. "Fair enough." He took a sip of his coffee. Tilted his head. Raised his eyebrows. "Hey, this is pretty good."

Not the exclamation I was hoping for, but at least he didn't hate it. I watched the nice fit of his jeans as he walked away, unable to help myself, and didn't pull my eyes away until another customer walked into my vision.

Chapter Two

THE COFFEE TRUCK STAYED intermittently busy, but I had enough breaks between customers to gaze around and take in some of the fair. Rachael's booth had steady customers, and before ten o'clock, she came over and said, "That's it. I'm out."

"You're out of paintings?" I asked.

"And canvases." She looked down shyly. "I'll have to bring more tomorrow." When she first showed me her artwork, she'd had a hard time believing anyone would ever want to pay for any of it, but she must have sold two dozen of her pieces tonight.

"Rachael, that's awesome! You should go have some fun and celebrate."

"Well, yeah. Ruth and the girls were waiting for me to go on some rides." She motioned to where Ruth and Sheena and a few other witches I was getting to know from the café were buying popsicles from the carnie with the red baseball cap who had seemed leery about my buying him an espresso.

Every time I'd looked over in his direction tonight, he'd had a lineup, and every time he'd seemed to have been splitting his time between serving customers and texting on his phone. He stuffed his phone into his jeans pocket, opened his freezer, and passed two of the witches a patriotic red, white, and blue popsicle. My dad, the senator, would like that—even if he didn't like anything else about me living in this town.

"I was wondering if I could stow my art supplies somewhere in your truck?" Rachael asked.

All of her paint pens were kept in a small fishing tackle box. It wouldn't take up much room, so I told her, "Sure. Marigold isn't with them, huh?"

Rachael shook her head. "No way. She wouldn't be caught dead here."

Marigold was known as the head of the witch group in town and ran the Witchy Wednesday gatherings at the café each week. She had a strong personality and had been loud and angry about being turned down for her own fortune-telling booth at the fair. There were hand-painted signs in the parking lot declaring "BOYCOTT THE WITCH-LESS FAIR!" but whether they were put there by Marigold or one of the other local witches, I didn't know for sure. Regardless, I felt a mix of pity and respect that she would miss the whole fair because of her integrity.

"But why is my cat here?" Sherlock had followed Rachael over and was now investigating the base of the coffee truck.

"He followed me from the marina. I couldn't make him turn back. I think he wanted to help."

I raised my eyebrows down at the squat cat. In truth, he'd become my best friend since I moved to Crystal Cove. When we were quiet together on the boat, sometimes I'd even hear his thoughts—although it had taken me some time to believe that was what I was hearing. But that cat knew things about my late Aunt Lizzie, parts of her I'd otherwise never get to know. He also had a good cat sense of who I should trust in this town and who I should not.

I sighed, making a show as though the cat was an inconvenience, even though in reality Sherlock was never a bother. "Okay, well, have fun!" I told Rachael.

Sherlock stayed with me as the group went off together and stopped at the nearby candy booth for Rachael to grab a snack. The carnie who worked there had also gotten an espresso from me at the beginning of the night. Sheena looked like she had ants in her pants, moving from foot to foot like she couldn't get to the rides fast enough.

Ruth bought a caramel apple with mini marshmallows on the outside that made my mouth water from forty feet away, but then my attention was on Rachael, who didn't appear to be in the same great mood from a few minutes ago. She crossed her arms and shook her head at Sheena. I wondered if they were arguing over which ride to go on before the park closed, but then quite suddenly Sheena stepped up to the candy vendor and purchased a large soda, which I didn't think would be allowed on any of the rides. She looked smug as she stepped away, and I wondered if this was her way of avoiding going on any rides altogether.

The witches in town argued a lot, so this wasn't unusual. When they disappeared into the fray in the direction of the rides, I figured they'd work it out and put them out of my mind.

Before the fair opened, I'd had a short time to walk around and get the lay of the land. The fairgrounds were large, but between the seven adult fair rides and the five kiddie rides, plus craft booths, a midway, and the food area, every square inch was packed. The midway was in view off to my left, and every so often, I saw a couple leave there with one of those giant life-sized teddy bears that a guy had won for his girlfriend.

I chuckled to myself as another couple I recognized from the café headed from the midway toward the hot dog stand with their giant stuffed animal. Walking around with one of Rachael's canvases would not have been nearly as much of a nuisance.

I looked around the base of the coffee truck and called out for Sherlock. He appeared from around the back of the truck, looking up at me through the coffee window. "I was wondering if you were still here."

More interesting than the empty boat, came into my head.

"Right. Well, don't let Mr. Klaus see you. He's kind of a grump, and I'll bet he doesn't have much patience for animals roaming around the fair without their humans."

Sherlock sat on his haunches and licked a front paw, appearing unbothered by this.

"How are sales?"

I jumped at my boss's voice, wondering how long she had been standing in the doorway of the coffee truck. Had she heard me talking to my cat? But if she had, she didn't let on, climbing aboard and joining me by the window. Thankfully, Sherlock knew what was good for him and disappeared behind one of the truck's wheels.

The fair was set to close at eleven, only half an hour away, so I had come to the conclusion that I probably wasn't going to get a break tonight.

Olivia looked over the till records, taking in the night's earnings. "Wow, it looks like you've been busy."

"Yeah, not too bad," I told her. "The fair's coffee specials were a hit."

"Why don't you show me the recipes for them and then you can head off. I'll close up here."

"Are you sure?" I asked, even though I didn't expect many more customers at this hour and I was quite excited to see if I could go catch up with Rachael and Ruth and the others. Their local witch group was definitely out of my element. Their focus was always on whatever supernatural magic one of them had induced, while I still had a hard time making myself believe that these all weren't just tricks of the hand or the eye. But I hoped that the more I was around the supernatural, the more I would be able to drop my automatic defenses and get my mind around it. Plus I really enjoyed their company when they were hanging out and doing something down-to-earth.

Olivia assured me I should go and so I didn't waste any time. I showed her the recipes and headed toward the rides. I looked around to find Sherlock, but he was staying out of sight. Probably for the best, as Olivia wouldn't have much patience for him hanging around either.

On my way across the fairgrounds, I passed a tall, lanky guy who was struggling under the awkwardness of one of those giant teddy bears all on his own. I wondered if it made him feel masculine, walking around with such a big prize, even though he had no one to give it to.

My stomach grumbled as I made my way through the rest of the food booths, but it seemed as though many of them were in the process of shutting down. Olivia would never have allowed that with the coffee truck, even though our whole area was deserted by this time.

I looked at the long lineup as I finally made it to the first ride, the bumper cars, and wondered if I'd even get a shot on it. This was only Thursday, though, I reminded myself. I had two and a half more days to try and squeeze in a ride or two. But weekends were busy at the café, and who knew how much Olivia would be able to get away to relieve me. Besides, the hype of seeing my new friends off having fun gave me a strange kind of nostalgia for something I'd never actually had.

I'd had friends in Portland, of course. But they weren't the same kinds of friends as I'd made so automatically since arriving in Crystal Cove. They were more like the kind of friends you were always trying to prove your worth to—similar to how I felt with my father, now that I thought about it. It was all fairly exhausting.

I passed the fun house, which had a rope across the entry announcing it was CLOSED FOR TECHNICAL PROBLEMS. I understood technical problems on a roller coaster or even a Ferris wheel, but what could go wrong in a fun house?

As I passed the carnie manning the closed entryway, the guy with the blue stripe in his hair, I called out to him to ask. "What can go wrong in the fun house?"

The guy shook his shaggy head and chuckled. "Have you been in ours? It's pretty good. We keep the mirrors super clean to confuse people, but every once in a while, someone gets dizzy and pukes from it." The walkie-talkie on his hip crackled to life, a voice on there saying something about the midway booths closing up for the night. All the carnies I'd seen today had walkie-talkies on their hips, and I wondered if Mr. Blue Hair had made an announcement to his coworkers about the mess in the fun house.

"Really?" I shuddered, thinking of the poor carnie who had to clean that up, which didn't seem to be Mr. Blue Hair, as he was standing around like he had nothing better to do.

"It'll be open again first thing tomorrow," he assured me.

I moved along past the roller coaster, which had twice as long of a lineup as the bumper cars, and the carousel, which had no lineup, but it appeared to be closed down as well. I was thinking it was awfully late for the kiddie rides, and maybe all of them closed down early, but then I saw an electrician behind the operating booth, shaking his head at a carnie, and wondered if there were technical problems there as well.

This was confirmed when the carnie's walkie-talkie crackled and a voice said, "You get that carousel up and running yet?"

As he pulled the walkie from his hip to respond, I turned in a circle, wondering where I should go next. I was willing to bet Rachael and Ruth were undaunted by the roller coaster line, and even with the size of Sheena's drink, she'd probably be finished it by the time she made it to the front. I couldn't see them, but the line wound around the ride, so not all of it was in view.

I sighed and turned to survey the rest of the rides once more before heading back to help Olivia clean up. That was when a hand in the air caught my attention from across the fair. That blond hair and those eyelashes were recognizable even from fifty feet away.

Jay. And he appeared to be by himself, near the front of a very long line to the Wave. Speaking of waving, a second later, he was waving me over. I wasn't one to butt into line, even if that was my favorite fair ride, but I felt strangely drawn to him. I went over to say hello before it was his turn.

"Come on, Tabby," he said when I was barely close enough to hear. "I need a riding partner."

I looked behind him in line. One of the guys slapped him on the back and said something I couldn't hear. The others all around him looked unbothered by the prospect of me darting into the lineup. Still, I asked, "Are you sure it's okay?" to the group in general.

The guy behind Jay unhooked the rope that designated the lineup to let me through. I supposed it was settled. I couldn't help but smile as the ride opened to let a new batch of riders on, and we were among the lucky ones. When I first moved to town, I'd been so worried about locals finding out my dad was a senator, but nobody seemed to care. It was as if Crystal Cove was a tiny hideaway, not actually connected to the rest of Oregon. I was still having trouble getting used to the small town niceties, even though I came across them almost every day.

We got into our ride car and I took the outside, well aware that if I were on the inside, I'd be squished like a month-old tomato by the time the ride was done. Seconds later, we brought our bar down in front of us and the ride started up. Excited screams and shouts sounded from every section of the ride as it went faster and faster, and soon I was shouting at the top of my lungs, too. At first, I held onto the bar for dear life, trying to stay on my side of the car, but soon my arms tired, and I slid to Jay's side and right into him.

He looked over at me, beaming. "I love this ride!" he yelled over the loud excited shouts and pop music. I nodded in response, but my throat was already parched from screaming.

Too soon, the ride slowed and then came to a stop.

We followed the line of laughing people toward the exit. "That was so great!" I said to Jay.

Jay nodded in agreement. When we arrived at the exit, he put a hand on my lower back and steered me to the left. "Let's go this way."

I did as he directed, but I couldn't help looking back. That was when I saw Detective Aaron Thom, another local from the police department I'd become friends with since arriving in town. He stood out, wearing his detective suit in the midst of the casual fairgoers.

"Is he working here?" I asked Jay quietly, even though Aaron was too far away to hear us. He hadn't seemed to have seen us yet, either.

Jay rolled his eyes. "Thom's always working. But no. Not officially, as far as I've heard."

I'd detected a slight rivalry between the two detectives since my arrival in Crystal Cove. Besides the fact that these two men had both asked me out on dates, Aaron Thom was the type of detective who liked to rely on only cold hard facts when it came to his investigative work. Jay went more by things like gut feelings and the possible magic that emanated from this town. Back when I lived in Portland, if you'd told me I would've come around to Jay's way of thinking, even a little bit, I'd have thought you were crazy.

But so many things had changed since then.

And as if to cement this point, Jay pulled something from his pocket. It looked like a small evidence baggie. I looked up at him in question.

"I don't know if you want this back or not, but I put in a request to get it released from evidence."

The slight blue hue that showed through the bag's labeling suddenly made my heart beat faster. "Is it . . .?" As I tried to get my question out, something rubbed up against my shins. I looked down to see Sherlock.

Jay nodded, not noticing my cat. "It's the blue crystal Rachael took from your aunt's houseboat. Rightfully, it belonged to Lizzie, which means now it belongs to you and your family." He held the small baggie out toward me, but I hesitated. He surveyed me for a long moment before adding, "I can keep it in the lockup, if you'd prefer?" He raised a questioning eyebrow. He was incredibly sensitive, understanding my struggles to believe in the supernatural, even if he seemed to have believed in it his whole life.

But when he started to pull the crystal away and slip it back into his pocket, I couldn't help myself. I reached for it. "No, no. I'll take it. I just . . ." I had no idea how to finish that sentence, so I didn't try.

I slipped the baggie into the pocket of the light jacket I'd thrown on, but having it suddenly so close to me brought with it a new emotional weightiness. I wondered if I hadn't been drawn across the fairgrounds toward Jay earlier but had actually been drawn to the crystal in his pocket. It wouldn't have been the first time I'd felt the pull from a blue crystal.

"The Ferris wheel line wasn't too long last I saw it," Jay said, breaking me from my thoughts. "You want to go?"

Jay had been backing off, dating-wise, and treating me just as a friend, while Aaron boldly asked me out every time I saw him. And since Jay had just gone on my favorite ride, I felt like I owed it to him to go on what seemed like his favorite.

"Sure. Okay," I said, glancing around to make sure we were out of Aaron's view and that Rachael hadn't appeared anywhere within my vision. She hadn't.

As we started to walk, I almost tripped on Sherlock, who seemed to want to continue weaving in and out of my legs, even as I was walking. I gripped the blue crystal in my pocket, pretty sure that he was feeling the strange pull of it the same way I was. I still had the urge to give it back, but somehow deep down, I knew I shouldn't. Instead, I scooped Sherlock up into my arms, hoping we wouldn't pass Mr. Klaus.

"You bring him everywhere you go, huh?" Jay sounded impressed, rather than dumbfounded, by my irrational habits. Then again, he had always liked Sherlock and even had the sense that Sherlock was more than just your average cat.

Still, at least I had an excuse tonight. "Actually, Rachael brought him after she was done cleaning the houseboat rentals."

Jay was right. The lineup to the Ferris wheel wasn't too bad at all. Unfortunately, this ride took a lot longer to board because they had to do it car by car. I set Sherlock under a bench near the entrance and told him to stay, without much confidence that he would.

Once in line, a young couple a few places in front of us waved to the carnie at the front and the girl asked, "Can we have the car with the teddy bear?"

I looked up to see what she meant, and sure enough, there was one of those life-size teddy bears in one of the Ferris wheel cars, just rounding the top. The two teenage girls who were in the car with it were leaning back against the teddy and taking selfies with one of their phones. Was the teddy bear permanently on that car and didn't belong to the two girls?

The carnie grumbled something toward the couple in line that I couldn't hear.

"That's cute." I motioned to the bear and told Jay, "But I'd think it would be a logistical nightmare for the attendant if everyone wanted to ride with it. Why do you think they did that?"

Jay shrugged. "I don't know. Maybe some rider just got tired of hauling it around and left it here."

I thought again of the lanky guy who had been struggling under the awkwardness of his large prize.

As the attendant began to switch riders to the next group of patrons, the couple in front of us stood aside to wait for the car with the bear. The girl was in her twenties with long dark hair, and she fixed her makeup with a small handheld mirror, I supposed getting ready for her own selfies with the bear. She looked familiar from the café, and I was pleased with how many locals I was beginning to recognize, unlike in Portland where every person was just another face in the crowd.

The carnie let several people go in front of the couple to fill the bearless cars. Other couples asked if they could come back and have a turn on the teddy bear car. We were right behind the lucky couple who'd asked first as the car with the bear arrived.

Now that I saw the teddy close up, it didn't look quite as impressive. The white bear looked as though it may have been dragged through the fairgrounds to get it here and even had some sticky, dirty-looking candy or caramel apple remnants around its neck. Suddenly, I could see why someone had left the big bear behind. I wouldn't have a place for such a large stuffed animal on my aunt's small houseboat, that was for sure.

But then a guy behind me called out to the carnie, "My girlfriend wants to ride with the bear. I'll give you twenty bucks for it."

The guy in front of us with the dark-haired girl wasn't a beefy guy by any means, yet his immediate scowl and puffed-out chest told me he wasn't going to give in easily. "No way! He told us we could have this round. You can wait for the next one."

He guided his girl toward the platform where the car had now emptied of people, but the guy behind me, much more heavily muscled, pushed past me and Jay. I didn't recognize him, but a lot of tourists came through Crystal Cove, especially in the summer. Renting the houseboats was giving me a better feel for local tourism and how many of them were looking for unforgettable experiences. I unthinkingly fiddled with the blue crystal in my pocket, still inside the baggie. If it really was magic, maybe it could somehow calm this situation down.

But the beefy guy kept barreling forward.

Jay let out an almost inaudible sigh and pulled out his cell phone. I wondered how often he went out just to have fun and was interrupted with a brawl that broke out or other police work to deal with.

But before Jay even had a chance to dial, the carnie threw up his hands and said, "I'm sick of this! People leave their dumb prizes on the ride and then I gotta deal with everyone fighting over them. The bear's coming off right now! No one gets to ride with it!"

People who had already loaded onto cars watched from above. The two couples in front of us tried to argue, but the carnie wasn't having any of it. He marched for the bear, jammed his hands under the bear's arms, and pulled back.

Nothing happened.

"What the . . . ?" the carnie muttered.

He bent deeper to put more weight behind his lift. I wondered if someone had glued the bear to the seat as a practical joke. But the carnie gave a heftier pull, and while the bear still barely moved, the head came loose off and tumbled off the Ferris wheel car and to the ground.

The shrieks that sounded all around made me look from the tumbling bear head back up to the rest of the bear. Inside what was more of a bear suit than a stuffed animal was none other than the angry businessman who'd brought the fair to town, Bryan Klaus.

His head was cocked awkwardly to the side. What I'd thought was dirty caramel apple on the bear was more likely dried blood from this man's neck.

And he didn't appear to be breathing.

Chapter Three

"STEP BACK!" JAY said from beside me an instant later. "I'll have to ask everyone to please step back!"

I immediately pulled my hand from my pocket, my fear of magic and of what might have happened to the fair manager automatically mixing together.

The carnie running the Ferris wheel, a short guy carrying an extra twenty pounds, backed away and glanced at his hands, which had fresh blood on them that looked nothing like dried candy bits. "What? Who would do this?"

"Sir, I'll have to ask you to shut down the ride." Jay turned toward the lineup of stricken people. "I'm afraid this ride is closed. If you have any information about this incident, I'll ask you to remain outside the ride entry. Otherwise, I'll need you to clear away and give us some space." To me, Jay turned and said in his all-business tone, "Can you go get Detective Thom? Tell him what's happened?"

I nodded, even though I felt like I could barely bring myself to leave his side. Erratic and overlapping thoughts about how this could have happened filled my head, and I was barely able to concentrate. The blue crystal was playing with my head. It had to be. Now more than ever I wanted to give it back, but there were more important things to do at the moment. Go get Aaron, I repeated to myself over and over again, needing to focus on the single directive, so as not to be overwhelmed.

The people from the lineup weren't moving very quickly, so I darted between them to get out of line and toward where I'd last seen Detective Thom. Suddenly,

Sherlock was at my feet, running his little legs off in trying to keep up.

"Did you see anything?" I murmured to my cat, still looking ahead in hopes that no one would catch on to who I was actually speaking to.

The answer that came wasn't from Sherlock.

"Tabby! Did Olivia finally give you a break to enjoy the fair?" Rachael's voice was bubblier than I'd ever heard it. She clearly hadn't heard about what had happened at the Ferris wheel.

"You should come on the tilt-a-whirl with us," Ruth suggested. Ruth had been one of the hardest witches to get to know in Crystal Cove. It was with good reason. She had a past she was trying to overcome and most often made an effort to fly under people's radar. Any other time, I would have been happy to have gotten this kind of invitation from her, but at the moment, my mind was getting derailed by thoughts of giant teddy bears and the blank look on Bryan Klaus's lifeless face.

"Have you seen Detective Thom?" I asked, looking around the whole group of witches.

Rachael's excited demeanor faded as she noticed my seriousness. "I think I saw him near the roller coaster. Why?"

"There's been an . . . incident," I said, having trouble coming up with another word for it. "At the Ferris wheel."

Unable to help myself, I started fiddling with the crystal in my pocket and had to close my eyes for a second at all the erratic thoughts that hit me at once. Another murder. I was right there. Why did this have to happen? Why did I have to see it? Why can't I leave this crystal alone?

Rachael, unaware of my racing thoughts, grabbed my arm. "Come on." I'd been learning Rachael was nothing if not helpful. She'd spent hours fixing up the inside of my aunt's houseboat with me and wouldn't take a penny for it. My words, along with my serious expression, were all she needed. She led the way toward the roller coaster. "I'll help you find him."

On our way, the other witches tagged along and peppered me with questions about what had happened.

"What was at the Ferris wheel?" Sheena asked with wide eyes, as though she already might know.

"Did something happen?" another witch I didn't know by name asked.

I nodded. "I think someone was killed."

"On the Ferris wheel?" Ruth asked in shock.

Sheena and Ruth stopped walking, both of their eyes now wide.

I shook my head, not wanting to give them the impression that the rides were unsafe. "I think he was dead before he was put on the ride."

I'd been thinking about it as I rushed away from the Ferris wheel. Why would Bryan Klaus have put on a bear costume himself and hopped onto the ride? Could it have been some kind of publicity stunt gone wrong? With his brash, always serious nature, it was much more likely that someone else had disguised him and then left him on the ride.

Sheena looked surprisingly at ease with this information, while Ruth was still in shock. "Murder?" she whispered. "And you happened to be there when it happened?"

Oh, great. The Witchy Wednesday group had automatically held some mistrust toward me when I first arrived in Crystal Cove because of my proximity to another murder. This wasn't going to make me look good at all in their eyes.

But at least I had one person on my side who they trusted. "I was there with Detective Jameson when the body was discovered."

Rachael rounded the bumper cars toward the roller coaster lineup, then spun back on me. "What were you doing with Detective Jameson?" she asked in a hurt tone.

My hand automatically went to the blue crystal. "I— He was looking for a ride partner." As soon as I said the words, I knew they were wrong. The crystals

Sherlock wore might have had some positive effect on me, but this one only seemed to be knocking me off my game. I forced my hand away from my pocket, and my mind became clearer of what I should say. "I was actually looking for you," I explained.

Whether or not Rachael believed me, I didn't know because right then she pointed and said, "There's Detective Thom!"

I rushed on ahead toward him. He was looking off in the other direction, surveying the fairgrounds as if keeping an eye on everyone, so I caught him by surprise when I grabbed his arm. "Aaron! Something's happened on the Ferris wheel. Jay needs your help right away."

Aaron looked down at me with a stern brow. "Detective Jameson?"

The note of jealousy in his voice reminded me I should have called Jay by his working title. Besides this, Aaron wasn't moving. I had to make him see the seriousness of the situation, and quickly.

"Bryan Klaus was discovered dead in a car on the Ferris wheel," I explained.

The witches had followed us over, and whispers of "Mr. Klaus?" and "Are you sure it was him?" and "Was he really dead?" erupted from among them.

I nodded to Aaron, in answer to all of their questions. "He was dressed in a stuffed bear suit, as if to hide what had happened to him," I went on. "But it's a mess of people over there, and Jay—Detective Jameson—needs your help to investigate and figure out if anyone around there knows anything about what happened to him."

Finally, Aaron started to move. He almost tripped over Sherlock, who was in his path. With the cat's short little legs, I was suddenly afraid of him getting trampled by our brigade and scooped him up into my arms again.

Another murder? immediately came into my head. I was getting some idea of how the blue crystals my cat wore on both his collar and his eyeglasses affected magic and being able to communicate with me, but that was where my comfort level with blue crystals ended.

As I jogged to keep up to Aaron's long stride, I answered as though he had asked the question. "I'm quite sure he was murdered and then placed on one of the Ferris wheel cars."

Too obvious. Who would place him there?

"There were a lot of fairgoers walking around with those large stuffed bears. I'd seen them from where I was working on the coffee truck." I pointed back behind us.

Aaron nodded. "Could you identify these fairgoers?"

"Maybe, if I saw them again," I told him.

Cause of death?

"I have no idea. But there was blood around his neck."

Aaron's head snapped toward me, and I realized my mistake. I had gotten so comfortable answering my cat's questions as though they were the detective's, he'd caught me in a misstep.

And Aaron Thom was the biggest skeptic of all things magical in town. He would have no patience for a communicative cat, or a jewel in my pocket that was playing with my mind, no matter how helpful either might be toward an investigation.

"I mean the cause of death," I put in. "I was just letting my mind turn . . . speculating."

Thankfully, that was enough to put Aaron's mind at rest about my sanity.

Either that or he had his thoughts on more important things as we arrived near where the lineup for the Ferris wheel had once been.

Chapter Four

"WHAT HAVE WE GOT?" Aaron asked Jay in a terse tone the second he found him, where he was still investigating near the loading platform. "Am I to understand there's been another murder?"

In the time I'd been gone, Jay had cleared the area of patrons, the car with the bear had been cordoned off, and the carnie had gotten all the remaining passengers off the ride.

Jay nodded. "I've called Mick and he should be here soon." Jay glanced at me, and then Aaron turned, as if seeing me and the witches for the first time.

Aaron held out both flat hands to us. "Ladies, I'd appreciate if you'd clear out and let us do our work."

"Actually . . ." Jay started, which immediately garnered a snapped look from Aaron, who wasn't used to having his authority challenged. "Tabby was an eye witness, and I think we should keep the witches nearby, at least for the moment."

Aaron didn't hide his eye roll. I focused on not stepping closer to Jay as I felt that familiar pull again.

Instead, I squeezed Sherlock tighter in my arms and tried my best to be helpful. "I saw several people carrying large stuffed animals like that one . . ." I motioned to the one in the Ferris wheel car, where the head of the stuffed bear had been temporarily replaced, probably to keep the scene from too much added attention. The ride itself had been roped off thirty feet away at the entry to the lineup.

Aaron pursed his lips, looking as though he didn't appreciate my intrusion, and then turned his back on me and stepped right into my eye line with Jay. "Tell me what we've got so far," he said quietly, clearly wanting to keep the whole conversation from any other listening ears.

I wondered why Jay wanted the witches to stick around. Did this murder somehow involve magic? Or was he simply hoping that with enough prodding, one of the ladies might have some supernatural insight?

Rachael wouldn't, as she'd been struggling to find her way with her magical gifts and had gradually been losing confidence in most of her abilities. Ruth, while skilled, specialized in potions, not in magic arts like psychic abilities or otherworldly knowing. I didn't know the other witches as well, but I had some idea that Sheena was new to their coven and considered a baby in witchdom, and the other two ladies seemed more like observers than partakers at the weekly Witchy Wednesday meetings. It was too bad

Marigold Weathers wasn't here tonight. She seemed to be the most knowing of the bunch, but she'd claimed she wouldn't have been caught dead at the fair after being turned down at having her own booth.

I paused on that thought for a moment, knowing I should probably mention her possible motive to either Aaron or Jay. But Marigold had become a friend since I moved to town. I had to at least talk to her about her whereabouts tonight first.

I couldn't hear much of what Jay said, what with Aaron completely blocking me from the conversation and the witches whispering behind me. I turned to quiet them with a wave, but when I did, I saw the terse looks passing between them, as though they were mid-argument. Worse, if I had to guess, I'd say Rachael was getting ganged up on. She looked about to cry as they whispered angry words in her direction.

"Hey, Rachael?" I didn't take time to think about it, placed Sherlock down, and then pulled her aside a few feet along the empty roped lineup. This put me a little farther from Jay and Sherlock, and my mind seemed to clear. "Is everything okay?" I asked, even though it clearly wasn't.

She looked at her shoes. "I think everyone's just upset about Mr. Klaus." She dropped her voice even quieter. "And, well, they're probably worried because everyone knew we didn't like him too much since he wasn't letting witches rent booth space at the fair."

I found it interesting Racheal used the pronoun "we," even though Mr. Klaus had offered her booth space. I wondered if that was why the other witches seemed angry with her, because she didn't have the same motive as the rest of them.

But then Rachael said, "I think they're afraid I'm going to mention that to Detective Jameson." That made sense. Everyone knew about her crush on the handsome detective. Then she added, "But I don't have anything to tell him." She shook her head at the ground.

I felt bad for how much she'd struggled in trying to find her magical gifts and I still felt bad that I'd been having fun and going on rides with her crush earlier tonight, so the moment I came up with an idea that might make her feel a little better, I ran with it.

"Hey, Rachael?" She looked up at my face and then immediately down to my hands when I pulled the baggie from my pocket. "Detective Jameson returned my Aunt Lizzie's blue crystal to me, and I hate to admit it, but with my inability in the magical realm, it's really playing tricks with my head." She kept staring at the baggie as if in a trance. I doubted myself, but only for a short moment. Then I knew this was the right thing to do. "Do you want to borrow it for a few days? See if it helps with your magic?"

Her eyes came up to mine. "Really?"

I passed it over. "I trust you'll be careful with it." After the last time she'd had it and it had given her a near-death experience, I had no doubt she would.

She nodded almost hyperactively. "I will. I promise."

I glanced over my shoulder. "But maybe you want to keep it quiet from the others, huh?"

The witches could be competitive, especially when it came to magical wares, and I certainly didn't want this to start an argument. Rachael quickly agreed and stuffed the jewel away in her pocket.

When we returned to the others, it seemed as though Sheena and Ruth had grown quieter and were also straining to hear what the detectives were talking about. Rachael stood a little taller as she joined them. I moved closer under the guise of collecting my cat and heard they were still on the topic of the bear suit.

I decided to focus on that part, too. If they indeed came back to me for help with who may have been responsible for Mr. Klaus's death, and who may have been walking around with large stuffed bears, I hoped to have some answers.

Bryan Klaus hadn't been in a great mood tonight, despite the success of his fair, but then again, I had never seen him look anything other than unpleasant, so I wasn't sure that said anything at all about his demise.

I thought again of the lanky guy I'd seen struggling under the awkwardness of his prize bear. He hadn't been familiar. Even though I'd only lived in Crystal Cove for three months, I suspected he wasn't local. Maybe the reason he'd been struggling so much was not only because of the size, but due to the weight of a human inside the bear suit.

Bryan Klaus wasn't a large man—likely no more than five-ten and a hundred and sixty pounds, but I didn't think I'd have been able to carry him discreetly through a fair.

Then there was that couple I'd seen earlier with their large bear. I didn't know her boyfriend's name, but I thought the girl's first name was Lorna. And they were definitely local, as I saw them regularly at the café. Hopefully either

Aaron or Jay would know who I meant with only a description and a first name. Two people trying to carry a disguised human made a lot more sense than one.

But what about people with motive? Could there have been more folks who were angry about being turned down for booth space at the fair? Then again, that didn't seem like a strong enough motive for murder.

"And did you ask this guy when the bear first showed up on his ride?" Aaron asked louder, clearly wanting the carnie to overhear, but in his usual brash style, not directing the question at him.

Jay moved toward the carnie. "This is Wilson Wright. I've already taken a short statement. Apparently, it was busy around ten p.m. He had to temporarily shut down the ride because someone had thrown a jacket into the prongs in the middle. There was a mass of confusion—some riders wanted to wait around and hold their place in line. Others left and pushed their way out of line to catch other rides before the fair closed. By the time Mr. Wright had climbed the structure and retrieved the jacket, he caught sight of the bear on a lower car. Am I missing anything, Mr. Wright?" Jay asked the carnie.

"That's about it." The carnie smacked a wad of gum between his teeth, looking less bothered than I would have expected at having a dead body discovered on his ride. The carnies at the fair all seemed to be early to mid-twenties, but this guy was a little older, perhaps almost thirty. One thing they all shared, regardless of age, was a hardened edge to their demeanor—like they had all lived tough lives already.

"You don't think the bear was on the ride before you climbed up to get the jacket?" Aaron asked, the same question I was wondering.

Wilson Wright shrugged. "Like I told this guy, it was busy. People are yelling all sorts of things and I have lots to keep my eyes on when the ride's running. Can't keep track of everything, but I'm pretty sure that's when it showed up, 'cause people started fighting over who got to ride with it right away."

"Where, exactly, was the car with the bear when you first noticed it?" Aaron moved closer to the Ferris wheel car, looking it over but not touching anything. The car with the bear had the number twenty-three on its side. Each car also had a large plastic jewel on the side—pink, purple, or blue. Twenty-three's happened to be blue but was otherwise indistinguishable from the rest of the cars.

I glanced back at Rachael, wondering if I'd been hasty in passing over my blue crystal. Then again, the one on the Ferris wheel car was obviously fake, and ever since I'd passed the real thing over, my mind felt clearer, like I wasn't trying to organize too many thoughts that were hitting me all at once.

Wilson shrugged again. "I think it was in the next position." He pointed to the car that was next to come around for loading. It would have been well within reach for anyone who wanted to place a stuffed bear on it. "The arguing over who got to sit with it started the next round, but I just ignored it and put the next people in line with the bear, 'cause I didn't have time to think of nothing else."

"The ride keeps you that busy?" Aaron asked.

Wilson glanced at the control platform. "Well, yeah, and also the handle on the controls busted right around then. I had to keep my hand on it the whole time while the thing was running."

Aaron raised an eyebrow. "Which handle was that? And you say it just broke tonight?"

As brash as Aaron tended to be, he was thorough at this job. I never would have thought to ask these kinds of detailed questions, but when Wilson led Aaron toward the control panel and it became obvious how difficult it would have been to go back and forth between loading and unloading the ride and the broken control, it definitely seemed like it could be important.

"I think this may have been tampered with," Aaron called to Jay. "We should get forensics to take some prints when they get here."

Jay pulled out his phone and spoke quietly to someone, relaying details from the scene.

Aaron continued to investigate the ride control platform, being careful to look but not touch. Before he was done, Mick, the medical examiner, arrived and had a short conversation with him.

When Mick made his way to the large innocent-looking teddy bear, Aaron waved in our direction and spoke to Jay. "Go deal with your witches somewhere else while Mick figures out things here. And find out if Tabitha recognizes anyone who had been carrying a large stuffed bear."

He sounded annoyed again, which only made me annoyed. But as Mick started to remove the teddy bear's head, I realized that maybe I should be thankful instead of annoyed.

Did I really want to look into Bryan Klaus's vacant eyes again?

Chapter Five

Whoever Jay had called clearly had connections. As we left the lineup for the Ferris wheel and Jay led us around the fairgrounds between the rides and the midway, policemen were everywhere, directing the few fairgoers who remained toward the exit.

"I expect the person responsible has already left," Jay told me as the rest of the five witches trailed behind us. "But there were a few people carrying large stuffed animals that we contained near the fair entry."

"But if they still have their stuffed animals . . . ?" I trailed off when Jay nodded, getting my point.

"Yes, but we can rule a few of these folks out as suspects, and perhaps seeing them will jog your memory of others."

I'd been so busy at the scene of the murder, I hadn't even noticed what was happening at the rest of the fair. Besides the fact that it was past closing time, it made sense that they'd have to shut it down if a murder had occurred here.

When we made it to a small first aid shack near the entrance to the fair, three large stuffed animals quickly came into view. One was being held tightly by Lorna, the girl I recognized as a regular at the café. She looked afraid, like even if she didn't know the details, she knew something bad had happened. Her boyfriend sat beside her, his jaw tight, looking more annoyed than afraid. But they still had their giant stuffed animal, which seemed to rule them out as murder suspects.

I didn't recognize either of the other two couples, and I thought again about the single lanky guy I'd seen with a bear earlier. As I stared at the bears and Jay asked these prize-winners a few questions about where and when they'd obtained them, a flash of a memory came over me about the lanky guy. He'd had been in his early twenties with dark brown hair and a mustache, wearing a light blue polo shirt and tidy jeans.

I squeezed Sherlock tighter in my arms, searching my memory for more, and that was when it hit me: he'd had a tattoo on his forearm. I hadn't seen it well enough to know if it had been some sort of serpent or a skull. I'd only seen some kind of black markings along his arm, and it had occurred to me that he didn't look the type to have a tattoo.

Then again, what if it hadn't been a tattoo? What if the markings had been bruises from wrestling with a fair manager?

As soon as Jay dismissed the couples and we left the first aid booth, I told him I'd only recognized Lorna and her boyfriend. Then I added, "But there was one single guy I'd seen struggling under the weight of a bear. He'd had markings on his right forearm!"

"A tattoo?" he asked.

"Maybe. Or maybe bruises."

"And where, exactly, did you track this man's course? As far as you can remember? And what time did you see him?"

I figured I might have a stronger memory for the man if I walked back to where I'd seen him. Jay followed me, and the witches followed him. But it was a short walk through the empty food booths to where he had disappeared toward the rides. "I'd say it was just after it had gotten dark. Maybe around nine o'clock?"

Jay questioned me more about the tattoo as he led the way to a picnic table in the center of the nearly empty fairgrounds, but unfortunately, I couldn't tell him anything else. I looked to the witches, in case any of them had seen him, but they were all caught up in their own quiet conversation. All except Rachael, who was turned away from all of them with a slight smile on her face and her hand in her pocket. Oh well. It was probably better she was the one having trouble concentrating than me.

Sherlock squirmed in my arms as I sat, so I let him down on the ground. He hadn't "spoken" during all the excitement, but then again, the din had been pretty loud and I had been rather distracted.

He immediately padded back toward the Ferris wheel. Only a second later, when Jay started asking another question, I realized this deserted picnic table was likely not where the bulk of the information would be. Sherlock probably had the better plan.

"Did any of you have a sense about anything going on under the surface here at the fair tonight?" Jay looked around at the witches, taking their attention. But each of them, one by one, shook her head back at Jay. I'd had to nudge Rachael to get her to answer, but then she shook her head as well.

"We weren't here to practice magic," Sheena said with a slight edge to her voice. "We weren't allowed."

Jay nodded. "I understand Mr. Klaus hadn't rented any of the witches booths at the fair this year. Is that correct?"

"Rachael had an art booth," Sheena said, as though that proved all of their innocence.

Jay made a note. Perhaps my aim to keep Marigold's motive out of this for the moment was futile. Jay and Aaron clearly had much more skilled investigative skills than I had.

"But nothing to do with the supernatural?" Jay checked with Rachael.

She shook her head. "Actually, that part was in the contract."

At this, Sheena let out a huff under her breath.

It had taken some work to convince Rachael to apply for a booth for her art. I'd thought it had only been a matter of her insecurity keeping her from doing it, but I distinctly remembered that when she went to Mr. Klaus's mini golf establishment to apply, it was the one time I'd seen her not wearing her black-and-white striped tights. It had been the one time I'd seen her trying not to look like a witch.

"I tried to book a booth for my potions," Ruth said. "I even said I'd call them essential oils because I heard he'd already turned down several local witches from getting booth space, but he replied to my online application and said he had no space for scammers like me."

The others around the table nodded at Ruth. If any of them had applied also, they didn't pipe up, but it looked as though they'd at least all heard stories of other witches being declined.

"And was anyone particularly upset about not being rented booth space?" Jay asked.

Again, the witches looked at one another. Sheena said, "Not that we know of. Like I said, we were just here to have a good time." Her eyes went wide and innocent. Either she was covering up her own feelings or trying to cover for Marigold or one of the other witches who had been boycotting the fair. I looked to Rachael, but she still seemed off somewhere else, and I wondered if she'd even heard the question.

Marigold Weathers had been declined a booth, I was pretty sure about that. About a week ago, she'd swept through the café, neglecting to even say hello to me, nor did she order her usual cinnamon macchiato. She'd stormed to the back of the café and ranted to a handful of witches who were already up there loud enough that I heard the name Klaus several times.

Still, no one mentioned this upset by Bryan Klaus or Marigold's fury, and for the moment, I didn't either. At the very least, I knew better than to mention this in front of the others at the table. While they could be backbiting toward one another, especially when one of them wronged the other, when they were on the same team, they could also be fiercely protective of each other. I might mention my thoughts to Jay later, when I could get him on his own.

But it turned out I didn't get a chance to speak to him on his own again that night. Soon, he accompanied us toward the fair entrance.

All the booths were closed up and vacated by this time, as there weren't many stragglers left in the fairgrounds. One carnie in the midway was busy stacking small stuffed animals from behind his booth onto a large flatbed wheeling cart. It seemed he packed all the prizes away overnight, which made sense, as the fairgrounds, even with a security guard, would be impossible to completely police through the night. I'd seen several carnies wheeling carts earlier in the night as they stocked their prizes from one of the nearby carnival trucks, and this jogged my memory.

I held out a hand to stop Jay along our trek. "What if the killer hadn't been carrying a large stuffed animal?" I motioned to the flatbed cart. "What if he used a cart like that one to move the bear?"

Jay immediately redirected his path toward the carnie, then held up a hand, stopping the rest of us from following him over to question him. It was too bad the witches all still wanted to hang around. I didn't blame them. With something so shocking happening in their small town, it made sense they'd want to stay close and see whatever information came to light, but I suspected if it were just me and Jay, he would have been willing to let me tag along a little closer.

Before long, Jay returned to us with a page full of new notes. The carnie with dark hair halfway down his back looked unbothered at being questioned by a police detective, which made me wonder exactly how often these carnival employees came across such awful crimes in their business.

Even though I wasn't surprised to see the rest of the food vendors shut down and deserted for the night, Olivia's absence was a surprise. Her responsible nature usually made her the last person at the café, even when I was officially supposed to close. I expected her to still be here, especially with a murder having just taken place.

It made me think that either the police had somehow been able to keep the murder quiet—which would have been difficult with so many observers at the Ferris wheel—or the police had quickly forced all the booth attendants off the fairgrounds.

At the coffee truck, I surveyed the fairgrounds from the point of view I'd had most of the evening, but unfortunately, it didn't do much to jog any other memories. I'd been preoccupied with serving customers for most of the night while it was busy. It was more than conceivable that the murderer could have pushed a cart with three dead bodies in big bear costumes right past the coffee truck without me noticing.

Still, I mentally went over the details of the people I had already told Jay about. Because I couldn't see the Ferris wheel or any of the carnival rides from my vantage point, I didn't see how I could be of any more help, and when Jay led us all straight from the coffee truck toward the exit to escort us out, I felt like I hadn't added anything useful at all.

Chapter Six

As we left the fairgrounds, I said to Rachael, "I'll drive you home. Did you leave anything at the marina?"

Rachael had barely shaken her head when Sheena piped up. "I'm happy to take her. You look tired, Tabby."

I had wanted to talk to Rachael about the blue crystal on the way home, offer her one more warning to be careful with it, but I really was exhausted. So tired, in fact, that it didn't occur to me until after I'd waved goodbye to them and returned to the marina that I'd left Sherlock at the fairgrounds.

"Shoot!" I whispered into the night as I held my key out toward the lock on my aunt's houseboat. I sighed. I was exhausted, but I wouldn't be able to sleep knowing I'd left my late aunt's cat out in the middle of a murder investigation.

But as I arrived back at the entry to the dock, Sherlock scampered on his short legs across the parking lot from the direction of the fairgrounds.

"You found your way home," I whispered, stating the obvious. I was getting more used to having other renters staying in the houseboats at the marina and having to be quiet, but Sherlock let out a loud mreow, as though he hadn't gotten that particular memo. "We'll talk inside the boat," I whispered, hoping he actually would talk to me once we got there.

"What is it?" I asked the second we were both inside the cabin of my aunt's houseboat. I'd kept the décor the same as Aunt Lizzie had it and strode for the purple loveseat where Sherlock and I usually had our "chats."

But Sherlock moved to the stacks of detective novels on the floor, ignoring me. I thought I'd put those away on the bookshelf earlier, but again the exhaustion must be muddling my mind. The cat had tried to help me understand a murder case when I first came to Crystal Cove by leading me to a certain passage in a certain detective novel. In truth, I still wasn't convinced that he had any more insight into these things than I did. Nor was I completely convinced of whether the magical happenings I experienced stemmed from my aunt's cat or her boat or the blue crystals or all of the above. But I had heard Sherlock's voice at the fair tonight, away from the boat, so that had to mean something.

"Can I help?" I squatted on the floor beside him and moved book by book aside to let him see the next one underneath. I wasn't sure how many thousands of hours my aunt had spent reading these books to her cat, but he seemed to know exactly what he was looking for.

Eventually, he found it in a leather-bound edition of a detective novel titled A Clue to a Kill. I moved the book out onto its own space on the floor and opened the front cover for him. Soon, he used his nimble paws to flip pages. He leaned in close against each one, as though he could actually read it with his glasses in place. I doubted that he could, but not enough to bet my life against it.

"Finding anything?" Either my exhaustion or my impatience made me ask this when he stopped on one particular page for over a minute.

He pulled away and pawed at a passage. I'd been reading a chapter or two of his choice each night before bed. I couldn't keep track of the characters or stories at all, as he seemed to want to jump to a different book each time I read. He either knew them by heart or didn't care at all about the story and only wanted to hear my voice. I didn't think we'd ever read from this particular one.

I pulled it up onto the loveseat and started to read. "Detective Hammersmith didn't have much patience for informants who took too long to tell him what they knew."

I chuckled under my breath because Detective Hammersmith wasn't the only one. It would be nice if Sherlock just told me what he was thinking, instead of making me piece together his thoughts from cryptic passages of fiction.

"He leaned across the interrogation table, looked his informant squarely in the eye, and said, 'What do you know about someone sneaking into the back entrance of the hotel, Britton?'"

Britton really liked to stall and talked around the question for two pages. He didn't want this to come back on him, and the detective keep assuring him of confidentiality. When my impatience wore thin, I skimmed to get to Britton's answer, which finally turned out to be, "There were three of them, and they all looked alike, as if they were related.

I saw 'em when I was taking out the garbage, but I don't think they saw me."

I sat back to think about this and see if there was any possible way to connect it to the current real-life investigation. I had considered that it may have been a couple who carried a dead Mr. Klaus onto the Ferris wheel, but I hadn't considered the possibility that three or more may have been involved. With the word "related," I pictured a happy family of three—two parents carrying a large stuffed bear with what looked like sticky candy around its neck. Their cute little girl in pigtails wore a giant smile, unaware that her parents were actually carrying a dead body.

I shook my head at myself. I was too tired to come up with realistic possibilities, but I pulled out my laptop on my aunt's small round table and at least started a spreadsheet for the case.

I listed the most likely possibilities, all the way down to the crazy idea of the pigtailed little girl with her parents. I started with two or three people working together to kill Bryan Klaus and then throwing a jacket into the Ferris wheel spokes, after which one of them would break the control on the Ferris wheel and finally place a dead fair manager, disguised in a bear suit, on the Ferris wheel.

But I also listed the possibility of someone trying to accomplish all of this alone—using one of the carnival's wheeling carts to move the body around.

I listed all the fairgoers I'd seen with large bears, including Lorna and her boyfriend, and I even reluctantly added Marigold Weathers to the list of people with motive, but starred "Tattoo guy" and put him at the very top.

Now it was just a matter of figuring out who this guy was.

When I felt like I'd gotten all the information out of my brain and onto the spreadsheet, I looked over at Sherlock, who now lay on his front paws on one of the detective novels with his eyes closed. It appeared I wasn't the only one who was tired, but at the same time,

I probably shouldn't go to bed until I'd gotten some more information out of that cat. He'd given me reason to believe that while he may hold great insight into the world, his memory was more than a little fallible, and if I waited until morning, whatever intel he may have gathered tonight could be gone.

I hoisted myself away from the table and headed to the galley. I pulled out his kibble container and shook it. In the past, Sherlock had seemed readier to communicate with me on a full stomach. He opened one eye but didn't appear interested in eating.

"What, then?" I asked. "What will get you talking?"

Finally, he stood and padded through the galley and over toward the door that led to the upper cabin and my aunt's bedroom. He swiped a paw at the door.

"So that's it, then, huh?" I hated to admit it, but I liked his idea quite a lot. "We'll get more figured out after a good night's rest?"

Chapter Seven

I FELL ASLEEP WITH A Clue to a Kill splayed open on my chest. I'd read it to Sherlock until I fell asleep, hoping for an insightful dream, but I awoke in the midst of more of a pizza dream—it didn't involve the fair at all, but instead included me attending my high school reunion and being dancingly tossed back and forth between my two detective friends, Aaron and Jay. Meanwhile, my father, the senator, stood near the drink table, tsking and shaking his head at me.

Even stranger, my father wore a necklace made of what looked like sea glass around his neck. As I chuckled at the dream and shook my head, a far-off memory came to mind and I darted up into a sitting position to process it.

Sea glass. My dad. It surely didn't have any significance to this case, but I'd completely forgotten about that piece of green sea glass my aunt had given me the last time I visited her when I was only eight years old. She'd said it was magical for me, or I was magical with it, or something like that. It hadn't been flashy or angular like the blue crystals, but rather smooth and calming. I'd tried to tell my parents about it when they picked me up from the houseboat, but my dad had gotten angry, taken the sea glass from my hand, and thrown it into the ocean.

Wow, I hadn't thought about that memory in years. I suspected I'd only dreamed about it now because my dad was still angry about me moving to Crystal Cove and getting my mom on my side about not selling my aunt's boat just yet. For the most part, from day to day, I was blocking my father's anger the same way I'd blocked it all those years ago when he threw away my sea glass—by simply putting it out of my mind.

And so now, apparently, all my stress was coming out in my dreams.

Still, I couldn't get it out of my mind, and as soon as I got up and dressed, I headed down to the rocky beach beside the boat launch to see if I could find a piece to reclaim a bit of myself—the part that I'd kept stifled under my father's close watch. I didn't have to live in fear of his opinions anymore, at least not while I was in Crystal Cove.

Sherlock followed me down to the shore and sniffed around the rocks as though he knew exactly what I was looking for. I wasn't sure where my Aunt Lizzie's collection of sea glass had gone. I hadn't found it anywhere while cleaning up her houseboat and packing up all of her personal items.

Sherlock pawed at a rock, and I went over to see that, sure enough, he'd found a small piece of pink sea glass. I picked it up and squeezed it in my fist, but I couldn't say I felt anything remarkable from holding it.

"Let's see if we can find another one," I told my cat.

We did. We found half a dozen pieces, all in different shades and colors. Sherlock had to point them out to me, but I hoped my eyes would start to tune into them soon as well so I could find a few on my own. Most of the ones we'd found so far were down near the shoreline, but I kept feeling drawn farther up, and so finally I went with my intuition, telling Sherlock, "I'm just going to look up here for a minute."

The rocks were of all different sizes, so walking on them was slow going, especially while looking for tiny pieces of sea glass among them. The sun had been shining brightly all morning, but as I took another step on the rocks, I suddenly felt its warmth come over me like a hot flash.

And then I saw it. A piece of green sea glass. I picked it up, and it was shaped almost like a heart, with a point that curved to the side. Right away, I felt a connection to it and told Sherlock, "I found it! I found the one I was looking for."

Even though my memory of the sea glass my aunt had given me so many years ago was faint, seeing this piece made me think it had been the same color. It felt familiar, too. It felt like comfort and a warm snuggly blanket.

My aunt had put a lot more stock into the magical powers of the common seashore knickknacks than I ever had, but the memory of my dad being so angry about my belief in them—maybe even afraid—made hope rise within me that I couldn't explain. Maybe it hadn't been a pizza dream after all.

I returned to the houseboat and dug into my aunt's packed boxes until I found one of her necklaces that contained a silver pendant with a purple stone in the middle that I'd seen when I was packing. I pried the purple stone free and wrapped it in a scarf before placing it back into the box that was earmarked for my mom.

Then I rifled through my aunt's junk drawer until I found some needle-nose pliers. Ten minutes later, I had the green sea glass situated in the setting around my neck.

As soon as it was there, I had the sudden urge to go back to the fairgrounds.

"Hey, Sherlock," I called. He was eating kibble in the galley. He looked up at his name. "Are you interested in tagging along for a trip to the fairgrounds?"

I suspected it wouldn't be open today. From everything Jay had indicated, it may not open again, at least for this year, especially if the investigation was elusive and there was concern for the rest of the town. As much as I understood this, I hoped this wouldn't be the case. If the summer fair was shut down and left on the note of a tragic death, what were the chances it would ever happen again? I'd heard the Crystal Cove Downtown Business Association had taken it on as a group in past years, but apparently with money shortages and disagreements over planning issues, it had ended up in the sole hands of Bryan Klaus.

I wasn't in touch with the whole town, of course, but from word around the café, I suspected folks had been a lot happier with the planning when the association had taken the time to hammer out their disagreements as a group. The lack of locals being able to book booth space was only one of the problems I'd heard about this year. In past years, there had also been stages and platforms for magic shows and other local entertainment that Klaus had cut from the roster. I wondered why that was and touched the sea glass at my neck. Would any of the witches be able to shed any light on Klaus's motives for cutting the locals out?

Sherlock didn't waste any more time eating and headed for the door, knocking me out of my thoughts and into gear. So it was settled. We were returning to the fairgrounds where Bryan Klaus had been murdered less than twelve hours ago.

If this sea glass indeed held any kind of magic for me, now was the time to figure that out.

Chapter Eight

WE LEFT THE HOUSEBOAT with me carrying Sherlock in my arms so as not to waste time waiting for his short little legs.

I was caught up in locking up and petting him and didn't notice the couple on the dock until I almost walked right into them.

"Oh! John and Julie Miller?" I guessed.

"Oh. Yes," John said, furrowing his brow from our near-collision, then immediately offering a smile. "Tabitha Chase?"

"That's right. You can call me Tabby."

"What a sweet kitty." Julie stepped closer and held out a hand for

Sherlock to sniff. "Oh, and he's wearing eyeglasses. How quaint!"

Because Sherlock tended to use other senses to judge people, he just looked down at her hand and then up at her face.

John and Julie Miller were my third set of renters in the houseboat next to mine. It was a popular rental, as it had floor-to-ceiling windows on the upper deck and new appliances throughout. The couple both had tidy blond hair and wore dress shirts and slacks, as if they were going to work and not on vacation.

"Are you in town for our summer fair?" I asked. Many tourists visited Crystal Cove for one of its local festivals or activities.

John looked at his wife and then back to me with a one-word question. "Fair?"

When Julie realized Sherlock had no use for her hand, she ran it over his fur. Sherlock could certainly be loving—when we were alone on the houseboat together or when he had some sort of investigative purpose. But it also wasn't unusual for him to take his time warming up to strangers. He snuggled deeper into my arms at Julie's touch, practically burrowing into my armpit.

"I thought there were no pets allowed," John asked not unkindly. Even though he still wore a smile, I felt the need to explain. I enjoyed elaborating about the house rental business, as I was still getting to know it myself.

"Each houseboat is different," I explained and was about to joke that mine actually came with a cat, but John was looking at the door of his rental like he was eager to get back to it. "I'm glad Rachael was here to let you in last night. You've found everything okay?" John stared down at his coffee, not answering, and his wife just stared at him. It was always my aim to try and help people see the beauty and fun of Crystal Cove, so before I even realized what I was saying, I told them, "Don't worry about the extra night. I had no one booked in, so I'll just include it in the price."

John continued to smile. If he nodded, it was barely perceptible.

They both had paper coffee cups from The Heirloom Café in their hands, so I figured I'd better let them go and enjoy them. "Do let me know if you need anything. I'm right next door." I motioned to the Lady of Fortune.

"But you're leaving?" Julie said.

"Oh, not for long. I'm just headed to the fairgrounds for a short time and you have my cell number if you need anything before I get back."

After saying goodbye, I crossed the street to grab a coffee from Olivia before heading to the fairgrounds. I'd invested in a coffee maker that was a little newer than my aunt's ancient, barely functioning brewer, but I rarely used it. Coffee, for me, had become a social drink. I spent most of my evenings chatting with locals as I served them at the café, so it no longer interested me to brew my own coffee on the boat and sit by myself to drink it.

As soon as I entered The Heirloom Café, the abnormal buzz was noticeable. I hadn't speculated much on how quiet the police had been able to keep last night's murder, but now that I thought about it, there were enough fairgoers in line at the Ferris wheel who would have seen the body of Bryan Klaus, and word spread too fast in Crystal Cove to keep something as big as this quiet.

I strode for the counter, which didn't have a lineup at the moment. Olivia turned from where she'd been working on her laptop on the rear counter when she heard my approach.

"Tabitha. I tried to wait around to talk to you last night, but the police were forcing everyone off the grounds. Did you hear what happened?"

"Hear it?" I leaned in closer and dropped my voice, not wanting to blab any details the police may have wanted to keep quiet. "I actually saw it!"

"What?" She met me at the front counter. "What happened? People are saying Mr. Klaus was found dead on one of the rides."

I nodded and decided to head back through the counter barrier to make my own coffee. Olivia wanted details, but I wanted caffeine. "On the Ferris wheel," I told her as I filled the espresso maker with freshly ground beans. "Jay and I were in line to board when he was found."

"Detective Jameson?" Olivia knew that we had become friends, but she kept her distance from getting too chummy with any of the local police. When I was first hired, she'd told me she believed in keeping on pleasant business terms with the police and not getting too close.

I had always refrained from talking much about my friendship with Jay because of it, but her eyes narrowed now, and I knew she'd want to know every bit of what happened last night.

"So the police saw it happen? Did someone actually kill him while he was on the ride?" Her words were little more than a whisper, and I found myself reading her lips to know what she was saying over the sound of the milk frother.

I shook my head. "They think he was already dead when he was left on the ride." I didn't know how much of this was public knowledge, but Olivia wasn't a gossip. She took in a lot of information about locals and tourists around town, and she wasn't one to spread it. With that thought, I figured it couldn't hurt to see if she knew anything important without even realizing it. "He was in a giant bear suit. It looked like a stuffed animal had been left on the ride, until the head of the costume fell off. Did you see anyone walking around with anything like that?"

She furrowed her brow, thinking. "Well, sure. Phil and Lorna had one."

Phil! That was his name. But we'd already as much as cleared he and his girlfriend from suspicion. "What about a tall lanky guy? He might have had tattoos?" When I was done frothing my milk, I motioned to my forearm.

Olivia's eyes drooped, as though my question made her sad.

"You know him?" I pushed.

She sighed. "Oh, yes. Hank Kessler's a staple around this town, but that family has sure had their share of struggles. I saw him heading out with a stuffed bear that he'd won for his niece last night."

"And he has tattoos?" I confirmed.

She shook her head in a way that I didn't think meant she was saying no. She went on to explain. "Hank has a blood disorder. He often has bruises show up out of nowhere because of it. A few years ago, he started getting tattoos, so it wouldn't look quite so bad. When his niece, Hope, got hospitalized the first time with leukemia, he had her name tattooed on his right forearm, to keep up the hope for her, he said." Olivia sighed again.

"That is a lot of struggles for one family," I said. "And his last name is Kessler?"

She nodded. "But if Bryan Klaus was in the bear suit, aren't you looking for more of a costume than one of the stuffed bears you can win at the midway?"

She was right. Up until now, I'd been wondering about which game vendor the stuffed animal might have come from, but this had not actually been a stuffed animal, even though it bore a strong resemblance to the ones being won at the midway. It was a costume. Which meant we'd probably spent a lot of time and effort on a worthless clue.

"Where would someone get a costume like that?" I asked, since she knew the town a lot better than I did.

"We have one dance supply store in town that doubles as a costume shop around Halloween."

That holiday was still months off. Still, I thanked her and said, "Hopefully the police will figure it out."

I didn't expect to hear much out of Sherlock since he hadn't seemed chatty with me last night or this morning, but once we were in the car driving south along the seaside road, some thoughts came into my head out of nowhere, which made me suspect they were from Sherlock's head and not my own.

Glass stab would make blood, yes?

I looked over to where Sherlock sat on his haunches in the passenger seat. "Yes, if someone was stabbed with a shard of glass, that would certainly make them bleed. Is that how Bryan Klaus was killed?"

No clues. No . . . remnant?

The last word came into my mind with a burst of confusion. I suspected Sherlock had overheard this word but didn't recognize it. Because I had no idea how he'd come about learning to communicate in English in the first place, I found myself relying on gut instincts more often than not when trying to have a conversation with him. "A remnant would be a piece of glass that was left behind in the body. Did it have to be glass? Could it have been a knife of some kind?"

I pulled into the nearly empty parking lot of the fairgrounds. Now only half a dozen police cars filled the gravel spaces.

Jagged cut. Could be knife. Could be glass.

"Is that what the medical examiner said?" Before I'd finished my question, I realized Sherlock may not know who I meant. "The man in the white coat?"

Only a guess, he said. Glass or knife.

When I went days or weeks without hearing Sherlock's voice, I always started to doubt that I'd ever be able to make it out clearly again. But then there were times like these, when he seemed to have so much to say, and it all sounded crystal clear in my head.

"So a knife or glass or something like it." As I said the words, a new thought occurred to me, one I'm pretty sure came from my own brain. "I wonder if it could have been a shard of mirror? Last night, on my way to the rides section of the fair, I'd passed the fun house, which had been closed because of a patron getting sick within the hall of mirrors. What if it hadn't been vomit but a murder that had to be cleaned up?"

As soon I spoke this idea to Sherlock, I couldn't shake it. It seemed like it had to be true. I had to tell one of my detective friends as soon as possible.

The entrance to the fair was blocked by yellow crime scene tape. An officer paced back and forth, watching for anyone who may not want to obey the tape. As soon as he noticed me, standing at the tape holding a cat, his eyes narrowed.

"I'm here to talk to Detective Jameson or Detective Thom," I told him.

"Are they expecting you?" I'd seen several of the local policemen when I visited the station to see Aaron or Jay, but I didn't know any of them by name. This cop had a shaggy mustache that looked like it would get in his way of eating.

I tried not to stare right at it. "No. But I may have some information pertaining to the case."

As Mr. Mustache backed away and held a walkie-talkie to his mouth, I realized it wasn't exactly information I had. It was a guess. And this guess was based on information I'd garnered from my eavesdropping cat.

Oy. They were going to think I was crazy. At the very least, I hoped it would be Jay who came to speak to me. He at least didn't require thorough explanations of unexplainable phenomena.

But just my luck, a moment later, Aaron Thom strode across the dusty fairgrounds toward us. He was an even bigger skeptic than I'd been when I first moved to town. Honestly, whenever this cat didn't continually remind me there may be things in this world I didn't understand, my default was to revert back to my skepticism.

"Tabitha?" Aaron furrowed his brow at me and then scowled down at my cat for a quick beat. "Officer Grant says you have information pertaining to the case? If so, why didn't you tell Jameson about it last night?" As with when I'd first arrived in Crystal Cove, Aaron suddenly made me feel not only like an outsider all over again, but actually guilty of some grave wrongdoing.

I'd come to learn over the last couple of months that this was just his way of operating as a detective, and in fact, it was probably what made him so good at his job. Still, I hated when he aimed that disbelieving gaze at me.

"It's just . . . I just thought of it," I bumbled. "Is Jay here?" As usual, I wasn't thinking clearly when Aaron made me feel like I was under scrutiny, so it took me a moment to realize that asking after my other detective friend would only make things worse. A flash of my dream came back to me at the look on Aaron's tense face. The two detectives fighting over me on the dance floor and my dad watching from the sidelines. "I mean, since Jay was the one who took all the notes about what I'd seen."

This didn't improve Aaron's mood any, but at least he lifted the police tape, an unspoken invitation to follow him onto the fairgrounds. He didn't wait up for me but turned and took long strides toward the picnic table where I'd been sitting the night before. Three more detectives stood nearby, discussing the case with stern faces. They all wore their dark suit pants with blue dress shirts, sleeves rolled up as it promised to be another hot day. Aaron was the only one in his full detective suit.

I walked straight for Jay, and when he saw me, he pulled away from the other two detectives. He took a long interested gaze at Sherlock, and his openness gave me the confidence to start talking.

"I thought of something this morning that I thought I should mention." I had hoped I'd be able to get my idea out without Aaron around, but he stuck close by my side, standing a little taller as we got closer to Jay.

"Someone else with one of the stuffed bears?" Jay asked.

"Well, yes. But now that you mention it . . ." I stopped myself before mentioning

Olivia's name. Not only would she not want to be brought in on the details of this investigation, but the detectives would also likely be unhappy with the idea of me blathering on about the case to the local café owner, even if she was my boss. "I was thinking about that, and wouldn't we be looking more for a costume than for an actual stuffed bear won as a prize?"

Aaron let out an aggravated huff. "She's right. That was all a waste of time." He shook his head at Jay as though it had been all his fault.

I felt bad for bringing this up in front of Aaron, and so I rushed on to say, "But I did figure out who the tall lanky guy with the bear was." Even though this was likely a moot point, Aaron and Jay both looked at me, waiting. "Hank Kessler?" I asked as a question. "Apparently, he's a local?"

Aaron let out another huff, shook his head, and moved back toward the other detectives, as if he didn't even have to express how little help I'd been and how much time Jay had wasted on this case so far.

Jay was much friendlier about it. "I'll bet he won it for Hope, didn't he?"

I nodded. "That was word around town." I still hoped to keep Olivia's name out of it, but at least if Jay asked for specifics, I didn't think he would jump to immediate anger about it. I quickly moved onto my next point, wanting to find some area I could help and not just shoot down all the investigative work they'd done so far. "But there's something else." I had his attention. "As I left the coffee truck last night and headed through the fairgrounds, I noticed that the fun house was roped off." I motioned in that direction, as the entrance was barely visible from where we stood. "I asked the carnie running it what could go wrong in a fun house, and he said someone had gotten sick in the hall of mirrors."

As I stared toward the fun house, I remembered the unwanted visual that had come into my mind when he told me this—a mess of undigested cotton candy and candy apple among the mirrors—and that gave me an idea.

I fiddled with the sea glass around my neck, searching for the right words, and the stone warmed between my fingers as they came to me. "When I first saw the large stuffed animal on the Ferris wheel, I'd thought it had held sticky remnants of caramel or candy apple around its neck, and well, I wondered if maybe someone hadn't actually gotten sick in the hall of mirrors."

I finally took a breath and looked between the silent detectives. Aaron had wandered back over to listen, as though he knew I was finally contributing something useful. I didn't want to come right out and say that maybe it was a shard of mirror, rather than the shard of glass they were looking for, because how would I explain knowing the murder weapon?

"It's certainly out of the way of spectators," Jay finally said. "I think one of us should check it out." He motioned his chin toward the fun house.

Aaron looked between me and Jay and then said, "Take Vickers with you," motioning to one of the other detectives.

After they disappeared, I didn't want to leave just yet, so I tried to think of a quick reason to stick around and see what Jay came back with. "Did you question all the carnies thoroughly last night?"

Aaron nodded. "Some of them left before we could get to them, but we have an officer over at the campground checking in with them today."

"They're staying at Camperland?"

He nodded. "They've taken over the whole place. At least we have them all together."

"Right. Well, the carnie watching the fun house had shaggy blond hair with a blue streak down the side." I motioned to my own red hair with my hands. "I'd definitely ask him more about the fun house closure. I mean, if you think it's important."

Aaron nodded. "It might be. Listen, I should probably talk to the other detectives and see where we're at. If you're going to stick around, I'd appreciate you staying put here." He motioned to the picnic table. At least he was giving me the choice.

"You bet," I told him and waved him toward his coworkers.

As soon as I took a seat, Sherlock wanted out of my arms. I let him down, keeping my gaze on the nearby group of detectives. I couldn't hear what they were saying from the picnic table, but Sherlock wasn't new at this investigation stuff. He immediately wandered a few feet closer to eavesdrop.

I pretended to check my phone so they might not notice my cat's lurking. I caught the odd word—Aaron's mention of the campground, another detective brought up the lab—but nothing that added to my understanding of the case.

I had one new text on my phone from Frank, who ran the marina.

~You might want to think about adding some lighting to the docks. As I was leaving last night, I heard a shriek and saw one of your renters almost fall into the water on her way out. Good thing her husband was there to catch her.~

I wondered why John hadn't mentioned this earlier. Then again, the Millers were so nice, they probably just didn't want to make waves, so to speak. Rachael had let them in last night well before dark. They hadn't known the fair was going on, and almost everything else had shut down for the fair, so where had they even gone to after dark last night?

I shook my head at the text, though. Shouldn't it be Frank's responsibility to add lighting to the docks if they needed it? Then again, Frank had made it clear when he first offered to get me in touch with the owners who wanted to rent out their houseboats that I would have to take care of hiring out all maintenance and repairs myself. The fact that he hadn't already added any lighting to his marina even for my benefit suggested he felt that fell under my responsibility.

I was lost in thought until Aaron's sudden louder voice brought me back to the present. "Hey, Tabitha? This is a crime scene. Not somewhere to let your cat wander, huh?"

I nibbled my lip and hurried over to grab Sherlock. If only I could explain to Aaron that Sherlock was actually trying to help with the investigation—and he might just be able to. I'd only known the cat for a few months, but it was already clear that his insight went a lot deeper than any of us could see.

But I also suspected Aaron's annoyance was only half about protocol. The other half was because he knew I'd been in line to ride with Jay when the murder occurred, after I'd told both of them I wasn't interested in dating right now. The thing was, Jay seemed to know how to back off and just be friends. Aaron didn't.

I was still near the group of detectives, retrieving Sherlock, when Jay reappeared, walking toward them and talking loudly. He, unlike Aaron, didn't feel the need to shield me from case details.

"No broken mirrors that I could see. If they'd replaced any in a hurry last night, I think we'd see evidence of that, but we could still have forensics take a look to confirm."

"So another dead lead." Aaron glanced my way for a second, as if to reprimand me. I retreated toward the picnic table with Sherlock, feeling bad again for wasting their time. I had been so sure this had been important.

But then Jay said, "Whoever cleaned up in there last night didn't do a very thorough job, though. Couldn't hurt to take some samples, just to be sure we don't find any traces of blood."

Blood? Had he seen something that made him think there could have been blood among the mirrors? Or had he, like me, first mistaken the blood on the bear as some sort of candy remnant and so he just wanted to be sure?

Either way, I had a gut feeling the fun house was important, and I was glad at least one detective was willing to take it seriously.

Chapter Nine

As soon as we were out of earshot, Sherlock let me know what he'd overheard.

Ferris wheel controls definitely tampered with.

"Oh yeah?" I whispered into my cat's fur. "So someone was trying to get Wilson Wright out of the way so they could get Klaus's body situated on the ride car?"

As usual, Sherlock didn't actually answer me. He liked giving clues, but I was learning that he didn't care for being interrogated. When I thought about it, throwing a jacket into the spokes of the Ferris wheel would certainly have gotten the carnie's attention away from the lower Ferris wheel cars; however, the control platform would have still been in plain view of at least a few patrons at the front of the line, so that part didn't make a lot of sense.

As the detectives ignored me, I tried to work through my own ideas. Who would have had a motive to kill Bryan Klaus? I hadn't known the man, but I'd heard he'd had contention with most of the local businessmen as well as the witches.

Who had the means? It would have taken more than one of the witches to kill Klaus, get him into a bear suit, and then place him in a Ferris wheel car. I was aware that the bigger part of me was looking for reasons they could all be innocent, but I couldn't help myself.

Who had the opportunity? Not Marigold, if she wasn't even at the fair. Two of the other witches? I thought of the group I'd seen the night before. They had claimed not to have been angry with Klaus, but I wasn't sure if I believed that. Still, wouldn't they have been avoiding the police, rather than following them around if they had actually committed such a brutal crime?

I didn't know any local businessmen, but I pulled up my spreadsheet on my phone and added all the ideas I'd come up with to investigate.

I stayed at the fairgrounds until I felt like I'd worn out my welcome. The detectives combed the area, taking photos and making notes. Aaron regularly peeked around rides and midway booths to see if I was still at the picnic table.

He had put Jay in charge of getting samples from the fun house, and by his tone when he gave him the order, I suspected Aaron wasn't putting any stock in it. Aaron needed Jay's help when there seemed to be otherworldly evidence in a case, things he didn't even want to understand, but when they were looking for cold hard facts, he tended to give him menial jobs.

I wished Aaron would allow me and Sherlock to look around. While I didn't have a lot of faith in my own ability to see clues that a group of detectives had missed, I certainly wouldn't have put it past my cat.

Aaron stared at me from behind another empty midway booth, where he'd been taking fingerprints from one of the large wheeling carts that the carnies had been using to move their booth prizes. He pursed his lips, and maybe I was learning to be insightful from my cat, because I had a clear sense that if I stuck around any longer, he would soon come over and ask me to leave.

I stood with Sherlock and offered a wave in his direction. "I don't want to be in the way," I called. "But call me if I can help with anything."

Aaron's eyebrows shot up, as though he was surprised at me leaving by my own volition. He was easy to read, but his attitude sure seemed to ping-pong back and forth. One moment, he was asking me out on dates; the next he was suspecting me of murder or angrily shielding me from the details of one.

I had decided not to date while I got my life in order, but the more I learned of Aaron Thom, the more I realized that while it was worth having a skilled detective in your corner, I wasn't interested in a relationship with him.

I wasn't as sure about Jay yet, although with his good looks, I imagined he'd be onto another pursuit by the time I was ready to move past friendship.

After leaving the fairgrounds, I went straight to Happy Hardware on Main Street. The clerk, CJ, who had been helpful with supplies for my boat repairs, led me to a selection of outdoor solar lights in the garden aisle.

"Did you make it to the fair before it shut down?" he asked me. CJ was in his sixties, and although I'd never asked him, he always spoke as though Crystal Cove had been his lifelong home.

I nodded. "I was manning the coffee truck there last night for Olivia."

"Shame what happened." He pointed to their selection of solar lights. "These usually stick into the ground," he explained. "But the dock has posts, right?"

I nodded.

"Tie one to each post. Just make sure they're not in the shade of any of the bigger boats. Then you don't have to wire anything in. Just replace the batteries when they start to dim, and otherwise they should recharge each day from the sunshine."

I was trying to pay attention, but ever since he'd brought up the fair, that was all I could think about. "You didn't make it to the fair?" I asked.

He let out a hearty laugh. "I'm too old for that sort of thing. But it sounds like I missed a boatload of excitement last night."

Excitement? Was that what he called it? I figured if that was how he saw it, it couldn't hurt to ask the blunt questions. "Do you know anyone in town who hated Bryan Klaus?"

Another laugh, this one more sardonic. "The easier question is probably who liked the guy. I know every time he was in here, he made me feel like he could take over Happy Hardware anytime he felt like it, whether I liked it or not."

"Is that right?" I didn't want to add CJ to my list of suspects, but then again, it sounded like I could add most locals to that list.

CJ waved a casual hand. "Ah, it's not as if we don't get our fair share of grumpy or entitled people in this store. Most times someone comes in, it's because something broke and people seem to think it's my fault or responsibility to fix it for them."

I hoped I hadn't come across that way about the dock lighting. "Well, you have a pretty good attitude about it, anyway."

He carried the solar lights to the till for me. "What choice do I have? But usually at least with the locals, I can get them to see I'm on their side by the time they leave my store."

He had certainly done that with me. "You get many out-of-towners?"

He tilted his head, thinking. "Not many. But, for instance, I had the carnival guy in here yesterday morning, angry because I couldn't cut a piece of mirror for him into an exact size."

I stopped pulling out my wallet and looked up at CJ. "Someone from the carnival was buying a piece of mirror? Yesterday?"

He nodded, oblivious to my sudden gravity. "That's right. Apparently one of his employees broke a piece while he was setting up, and he was none too happy about it."

One of his employees? "So do you think this was the carnival manager? The guy in charge of all the rides?"

CJ nodded. "That's what he said. He runs the rides, the midway, the food vendors, and he said something new breaks almost every time they tear down and set up. You'd think with so many problems, he'd have gotten used to it and not blamed the guy who could solve his problems." CJ pointed to his own chest, but I was lost in my racing thoughts.

If the carnival manager came in to buy a piece of mirror yesterday morning, maybe it was because he knew one would get broken later that night—one that was used to kill someone.

"Do you know this guy's name?" I asked CJ.

He didn't, but he described him for me. "Short squat guy, with a perpetually red face. The guy's going to have heart trouble if he keeps letting these day-to-day breakages get to him."

I wasn't worried about the guy's heart. There were other things that concerned me much more about this carnival manager.

I thanked CJ and left with my lights, still feeling like they should be Frank's responsibility, but more than that, not wanting Julie Miller to actually take a tumble into the water.

I didn't want to return to the fairgrounds without an invitation, so instead I sent Jay a text.

~Call me when you have a minute to talk.~

After stowing the lights in my trunk, I instinctively turned uptown, rather than down toward the marina. Dance Dance Dance was only a couple of blocks up. I figured why not stop in and see what they could tell me about costume rentals.

The bell jingled over the door as I entered, and the place appeared empty, other than the fiftysomething woman with a tight bun standing behind the counter. She looked up, smiled, and said hello as I entered, but her smile seemed tense, as though perhaps I was interrupting her.

"What can I help you with?" Her smile remained, but I couldn't tell if she actually wanted to help or just wanted to get back to whatever she had been working on behind her counter. As a senator's daughter, I usually recognized when there was something behind the smile. I just wasn't always the best at nailing down what it was.

"I have some questions about costume rentals."

"Ah, yes. We have most of our options here in this book if you'd like to take a look." She pulled a large blue binder from a back counter and placed it on the glass counter that separated us. "Are you going to a special party?"

"Something like that." I stepped up and opened the binder. It had at least a hundred plasticized pages, each with four costumed photos of people. The youth of the models and the way they posed made me think she'd gotten dance students to pose for most of the photos. "Do you know if you have any bears?"

Thankfully, this lady knew her business. She flipped about halfway through the book and navigated to a page she seemed to know well. When she turned it back to me, it had three children in bear costumes. Two were black bears and one was a more cartoonish-looking brown bear.

"Oh, um, I guess I'm on the lookout for something that looks more like a giant teddy bear," I suggested. "Adult size. And white." She looked at me blankly, so my next question seemed almost unnecessary. "Do you have anything like that?"

From her back counter, she reached for a glossy magazine. "We can order anything from in here, but I'm afraid I'm not entirely sure that we can get something so specific. You could try Costume City. They have locations in Seattle and Portland."

I nodded and flipped through the magazine in hopes that I wouldn't find any reason to have to take an immediate trip to Portland. "So you haven't sold or rented a costume like the one I'm talking about anytime recently?"

She shook her head. "I can't say I've ever even seen one in white. I'd think it would be hard to keep clean. And you say you're wanting it to resemble a teddy bear—like pudgy around the middle?"

I thought back to Mr. Klaus's lifeless body, shielded by the bear outfit on the Ferris wheel. "That's right."

She helped me find the section of the magazine that contained animals, but again, they were mostly for children and all the bears were of a darker shade. If the murderer had opted for a darker color, the blood certainly would not have been as obvious.

I tilted my head, letting that thought turn over for a minute. There was one adult bear costume that looked similar, but only came in black. Still, I pointed to it. "How much would one of those costumes rent or sell for?"

She turned the magazine toward her. "Oh, I would think most folks would rent, especially if it was only for a one-time event. We generally rent costumes for twenty-five to fifty dollars a day, but the cost of this one . . . ." She located an item code and tapped it into her computer.

"This would be almost three hundred to purchase."

"Hmm. Okay." I thought again about the blood around the neck. "And what if a costume like that got wrecked or was returned in bad shape?"

She nodded, as though this wasn't an unusual occurrence. "We take a hundred-dollar deposit. It often doesn't completely cover the cost of the costume, but that, along with the renters who do take care of their costumes, ends up working out in the end." She looked up and laughed, remembering something. "One time a local witch rented one of my clown costumes, and when she returned it, it was a dinosaur!" She laughed again.

I furrowed my brow. "Do you know who this witch was?"

The lady smiled and dropped her voice to almost a whisper. "I don't like to say, but it was Rachael Adams. I didn't keep her deposit because the dinosaur was actually a better costume, worth more, and it's one of the new favorites.

Besides, she seemed some upset about the whole thing."

That was true to Rachael's character. She'd been struggling to have her magic spells go the way she planned since before I'd met her. And a clown and/or dinosaur costume did not lend anything to this investigation.

The lady went on, oblivious to my mulling thoughts. "But I have to say, that's part of the reason I wouldn't carry some of these expensive costumes in my store. We do what we can to clean and preserve costumes, of course, but it's not always possible, and I have to turn a profit."

"Of course," I agreed. I thanked her and left the store, making a mental note of the magazine that sold those bear costumes, even though they did not have them in white. I made a note of Costume City on the spreadsheet on my phone so I could look up their website later. But then I also made a note beside the witches, with a new thought:

WHAT IF THE WITCHES CAST A SPELL TO CHANGE A COSTUME INTO EXACTLY WHAT THEY NEEDED?

As I headed back to the marina, I speculated more on who would have bought and/or rented a bear suit, because deep down, I didn't want to believe it had been one of the witches.

It probably couldn't have been a rental, I surmised, because the murderer clearly never planned to return it.

Chapter Ten

As I ATTACHED THE last solar light to a post on the wharf using some twine CJ had thrown in as a freebie, John and Julie Miller made their way from the parking lot and down onto the dock.

"I'm so sorry! I heard you almost slipped last night," I called as they moved closer.

"I'm surprised someone hasn't already sued over this." Even though John said this with a smile, or maybe it was because he said it with a smile, the words reminded me of my father. I tried to shake off that thought so my response wouldn't come out nasty.

"Well, it should be plenty bright enough by tonight."

"What do you think, Julie? Should we ask for a cash discount?" John chuckled, still with that pasted-on smile, so I couldn't tell if he was serious.

His question sounded like a joke, and at the very least was directed at his wife, so I didn't respond. Besides, I'd already comped them a free night when they arrived early.

This post was wider than the previous ones and giving me some problems with getting the twine around while securing the solar light up above the water. Mr. Miller saw me struggling but didn't offer any help.

"Well, there'll be light now," I said again in a forced cheery tone, then gritted out a groan as the light slipped once more and I barely caught it before it landed in the water.

When I looked up again, Mr. and Mrs. Miller had disappeared back inside their rental houseboat. I was about to attempt securing the light one more time when

I heard Frank's office door bang shut. Frank, the marina owner, was in his forties and kept a floating office near the land edge of the marina. He didn't spend much time there lately, as he kept pretty busy, especially in the summer, giving local tours.

"Hey, Frank?" I couldn't see his office from where I stood, but he must have heard me, as he poked his head around the corner seconds later.

"Tabby. What's up?" As usual, he had a hurried nature about him. I took care of a lot of the day-to-day details around the marina these days, even giving tourists information about his tours, and I figured he should act a little more appreciative. Then again, I had practically accused him of cold-blooded murder when I first landed in Crystal Cove.

"Can you just hold this light for a sec? It's my last one and this post is a bit too big to wrap my hands around."

Frank headed my way, surveying the other solar lamps I'd already secured on various posts. When he arrived at the large post, he pulled at the top of it, which appeared to have a plastic cover. All of the posts had little caps on them and I wasn't sure what purpose they served. I figured maybe they helped stop the corrosion from the surrounding water or something.

But once Frank had the cap removed, he took the lamp from my hand and stuck the pokey end that would normally stick into grass into the top of the post. It fit snuggly enough that he had to give it a shove to get it all the way in.

"Oh. Okay. Thanks," I said. I supposed it didn't matter if it didn't look exactly the same as the others.

"It'll get more sun up higher," Frank explained. "And burn brighter once the sun goes down." He seemed to know about all things mechanical or for boat or dock improvement. It was too bad he was usually too busy to help with any of it.

"I thought I should get something up as soon as possible so my renters don't fall in and try to sue." Even though I didn't see that as likely, I couldn't stop thinking about it.

"Ah, they were probably just tired last night. It doesn't get that dark out here, especially with the nice weather in the summer."

"What time did you see them coming back here?" I asked. Maybe it was my inquisitive nature, or just the fact that I naturally didn't trust people like my dad who covered most things up with a smile, but I felt the sudden need to look into my renters a little more closely. I'd much rather have reason to suspect people I'd only barely met of wrongdoing, people who seemed to be hiding something, than my witch friends. "And do you know where they had gone?"

Frank shook his head. "It was after ten and they were headed out, not back to their houseboat. Who knows what's open at that time besides the pub, but I didn't stick around to find out where they were headed."

I suspected the real reason he didn't stick around was because he didn't want to deal with apologizing to the lady who had almost fallen in. But if the Millers were headed out after ten, they may have been involved in something shady or secretive, but it likely had nothing to do with the murder of Bryan Klaus.

"These lights are great," Frank said. "I hadn't considered just grabbing some solar ones. Quick and easy."

It hadn't exactly been quick and easy for me. In fact, I'd spent most of the afternoon working on them. But I smiled my thanks, especially when Frank added, "Leave the bill in my office, and I'll take it off your mooring fees."

When I was finished, I went into the Lady of Fortune to wash up. I still hadn't heard back from Jay, but I was itching to do some more investigating. I pulled up my spreadsheet and immediately found the place I wanted to go to ask some questions.

Half an hour later, I parked not far out of town in a large sprawling lot next to Crystal Cove's only mini golf establishment. Bryan Klaus had been the owner, and while I had no idea who would own it now, I figured anyone working here probably knew more about the man than I did.

But the parking lot only held three other cars, so I had to wonder if it had shut down with its owner's death. I strode past a deserted outdoor course full of green ramps and obstacles and up to the front glass doors, expecting them to be locked, but one swung freely open under my hand.

I hadn't been inside Crystal Mini-Golf before, so I was surprised to see more than just stretches of fake turf in the interior of the large round building. There was a deserted mini golf course off to my left, smaller than the outdoor one, but to my right were video games, foosball, and Skee-Ball games. A mother and her two young children were playing Skee-Ball, so the place had to be open, but it was otherwise empty.

I wondered if the young mom hadn't heard the news about the owner or maybe she was from out of town.

The only other person in the place was a girl of maybe eighteen behind a counter that displayed everything from a hot dog machine to a selection of sodas, candy, and golf club rentals. I strode toward her, and when I got close enough, I saw her name tag read BECKY.

Becky was busy on her phone and didn't look up until I cleared my throat and said, "Hi there."

She glanced up, but only for a second. "Tokens or golf?" Her brown hair was in a ponytail, but much of it had come loose, and she wore a gray hoodie that was at least three sizes too big for her.

"Oh, actually, I'm not here to play." I paused, but she kept typing into her phone, apparently uninterested in doing more than just the bare minimum of her job. "I just had a few questions about your boss, if you don't mind."

This made her look up. Her eyes narrowed warily at me. "You a reporter or something? If so, I'll give you Mrs. Klaus's number. I'm not supposed to talk to reporters."

There was a Mrs. Klaus? I supposed that explained why the business was still open. "No, I'm not a reporter," I told her. "Actually, I was one of the first people to find your boss on the Ferris wheel and I just wanted to know a little more about him."

Becky looked at me side-eye, like she still didn't completely trust my motives.

I reached to my neck and held my sea glass, looking for the words that would make her trust me. "I was running the coffee truck at the summer fair. I work with Olivia at The Heirloom?" I asked it as a question. If she worked in town, she had to know of it.

She did. I could see immediate recognition on her face. "What do you want to know about Mr. Klaus?"

I'd written a slew of questions in my spreadsheet, but suddenly I had trouble remembering a single one. If I pulled up the spreadsheet on my phone, though,

I'd be sure to come off as a reporter. I squeezed the sea glass tighter in my fist and eventually came up with somewhere to start.

"What was it like working for the man?"

Becky shrugged. "I've only worked here a couple of months. I'm sure you've heard he wasn't the nicest guy."

"No?" I'd learned from Aaron and Jay to leave pauses, rather than immediately filling in gaps in conversation. Thankfully, it worked.

"Turnover in this place is crazy. No one lasts more than a few months. He's gone through so many employees from this town, it's amazing there's anyone left. It's what you get when you're a jerk to your workers." Becky looked at her phone again, as if to emphasize that even from the grave, Bryan Klaus didn't have much recourse if she decided to spend her entire shift on her phone.

"So a lot of people who work here or who have worked here didn't like the guy?" I confirmed.

This made her let out a low chuckle. "Put it this way, not a lot of people are heartbroken about what happened to the guy. Except maybe his wife."

This surprised me. "Is she here?"

Becky shook her head. "She's pretty stressed out, not only with her husband kickin' it, but now she's on the hook for the cost of the fair, which isn't bringing in any money. She's a mess over the whole thing."

"His wife really loved him, huh?" I wondered if I should ask for Mrs. Klaus's phone number but worried that might stop Becky from talking, so I didn't for the moment.

She shrugged with a look of distaste. "I'm not sure love is the right word. But they sure understood each other."

"You mean she's not a very nice person either?"

Becky huffed out a laugh and nodded.

"Is there anyone you know of around here that really hated Mr. Klaus? Like hated him enough to kill him?"

She raised her eyebrows, and this brought on a smile at the edge of her lips. She looked up as if she was thinking about it, but then she said, "Like I said, probably almost anyone. I think the more important question is who actually had the smarts to pull it off. I wouldn't think anyone around this place, that's for sure." Even though she said this, I got the distinct impression that Becky was smarter than she let on. Or at the very least streetwise. "If you really want to find someone who hated the guy and could get away with offing him, I'd look at the guys he's put outta business."

"He's done that a lot?" I asked.

She nodded with her eyebrows raised. "Not only that, but he likes to humiliate them first. Apparently, the guy that used to run a bar in this place was sued over everything from food poisoning to endangerment, all organized by Mr. Klaus, before the bank finally took it over and he bought it for a steal. At least that's the way the story goes. I even heard he blackmailed the guy he put out of business to dress up as his mascot for the mini golf's grand opening." Becky laughed and pointed to a wall at the end of the counter, which held a dozen photographs. Many of them were filled with smiling children, but I moved closer to see something else that appeared in each photo.

A life-sized white teddy bear.

I pointed to the photo where it was most prominent. "That's the mini golf mascot costume?" I pulled out my phone and snapped a picture of the photos, no longer caring if this made me look like a reporter. She'd barely started to nod when I had to ask, "Do you know where that costume is now?"

"Sure. It's in the back storage room." She motioned to a door behind the counter.

I sucked in my breath. "Can I see it?"

She looked at me with a twisted expression like she thought I was crazy, but after a long beat, she turned and moved through the rear door. Only seconds later, she was back with a large cardboard box. It didn't look nearly as heavy as the bears being won at the fair looked, and a second later, when she dropped the box on the floor and the top flaps popped open, it was obvious why. The box was empty.

"That's where the bear costume is usually kept?" I confirmed.

She nodded, then reached into the bottom of the large box. She came out with a small yellow sticky note that read: MR. KLAUS BORROWED FOR THE SUMMER FAIR.

I squinted at the note, snapping a photo of it as well.

"That's weird," Becky said.

At first I thought she meant me taking a snapshot of the sticky note. But when I looked over, she was studying the note closer. "What's weird?"

She shook her head. "This isn't Klaus's writing."

I questioned her about whose writing it might be, but she had no idea. "Do you know the name of the guy who had to wear this costume or who used to own this place?" I looked around, trying to envision the place as a bar.

Becky shrugged. "I heard the guy left town and hasn't been heard from since. But like I said, Klaus has done that sorta thing a lot. Put guys out of business so he could take it over real cheap and then resell it. This is the only place he hung onto, but I think that's only 'cause Mrs. Klaus likes the place. I'll bet there are a lot of people around town who've been celebrating his death."

I left Bryan Klaus's business feeling like the more questions I asked around Crystal Cove, the more suspects I'd be able to find.

Chapter Eleven

THAT EVENING I HAD the night off from the café, as Olivia had hired an extra girl to take a few shifts when she thought I'd be busy taking care of the coffee truck. But now with nothing to do and nowhere to go, I decided to stay in for a quiet evening with my cat.

Jay had finally texted me back and said he didn't have time to chat, so I relayed all the details I'd found out from Becky at the mini golf place and CJ at Happy Hardware via text, which got me thinking again about the manager of the carnival. Jay thanked me and said he'd look into it, but I couldn't tell via texting how serious he thought the sale of a piece of mirror might be as a lead.

I cooked up a stir-fry for myself on my aunt's hot plate and opened a can of tuna for Sherlock. He'd been stuck in the car for a good part of the afternoon while I went from the hardware store to the dance store and then the mini golf complex, and I'd promised him tuna for dinner on our way back.

While he loved tuna, he had a strange habit of taking his time eating it. I always placed the circle of tuna straight from the can into his dish, and he'd pry a single flake away with his front claw, place it beside his dish, and proceed to take his time looking at the flake from every direction before eating it.

Since I knew he'd be busy for the better part of an hour, I finished my stir-fry and took a cup of chamomile tea out onto the front deck to enjoy it.

The solar lights weren't exactly bright, but they added a nice ambiance to the dock. They would also aid the Millers on and off the dock if they chose to go out.

The lights were on in the houseboat the Millers were occupying, but I didn't see anyone inside from my vantage point. After moving onto my aunt's boat, I'd refinished the wrought iron chairs and table on the front deck with a wire brush and then sprayed them with some rust-resistant black spray paint so they looked as good as new.

In the daylight, they looked smart with the purple drapes my aunt had hung outside. The drapes were not my style, but as with most of my aunt's decorations, I hadn't been able to bring myself to change them. Besides, they blocked me from view from the rest of the wharf and it was nice to have the outdoor privacy whenever I had renters on the other houseboats.

Mr. Miller came into view through the window of the galley of the houseboat he was staying in. A moment later, Julie Miller also came into view, and while I couldn't see or hear them clearly, it looked by their flailing arms as though they were mid-argument.

I wondered again what had brought the couple to Crystal Cove. They seemed too young to be retired, but they also didn't seem the type to be swept up in the supernatural occurrences surrounding Crystal Cove. We got the odd tourist who just came for the beaches, but there were nicer sandy beaches just half an hour up the coast, so that wasn't common. Besides, something about the Millers made me think they were not here for simple relaxation.

I took a sip of my tea as they disappeared out of view again. I was about to head back inside to fill my cup when the slamming of the door on the houseboat next door startled me. It was Mr. Miller, and with the new lighting along the dock, I had no trouble seeing the hunch of his back as he strode purposefully toward the entry of the wharf and then beyond that to the parking lot.

I wondered if Frank was right and he was headed for the pub. Was he headed out to blow off some steam? Or did he have a drinking problem and that was what he was covering up with his ever-present smile?

He drove away in his car, and I hoped he wouldn't be driving drunk later. I felt bad for Julie Miller. She seemed friendly enough and reminded me a bit of my mother, who tended to try a little too hard to follow her husband's directions in order to keep the peace.

With a sudden idea, I headed back inside my aunt's houseboat. When I left The Heirloom Café earlier today, Olivia had sent me with a container of six cinnamon buns. Olivia's cinnamon buns were my favorite, with extra dollops of sweet cream cheese adorning each one, and she said I might as well take them, as they were already day-old and she didn't want them to go to waste. Even though I knew I shouldn't eat six giant cinnamon buns by myself, I couldn't resist taking them. And I'd already devoured two.

When I got to the galley, Sherlock was still working on his tuna. He looked up at me for a second and then went back to his meticulous tuna picking. I opened the box of cinnamon buns on the counter and wondered if I should deliver all four to my temporary neighbors.

But I wasn't that generous. I wanted to enjoy at least one for breakfast the next morning. Instead, I found a plastic serving tray in one of my aunt's cupboards and packaged two of them to go. I felt the sea glass around my neck warm, something I was starting to recognize more and more, and knew it was the right thing to do. Really, they were just an effort to make Julie Miller feel a little better, and I kind of hoped she'd help herself to both of them before her husband returned.

Moments later, I knocked on the door of the neighboring houseboat. I'd been inside many times while getting the vessel ready for renters. It shouldn't take more than a minute for Julie to get to the door, no matter where she was aboard the floating house, but when a minute passed, and then two, I knocked again.

Footsteps padded toward the door and then it opened, but only an inch. One of Mrs. Miller's eyes peeked through the crack. "Hello?"

"Hi, Mrs. Miller. It's just me, Tabby, from next door?"

She didn't pull the door open any farther.

"I had some extra cinnamon buns and thought you and your husband might enjoy them." I held the tray an inch closer to the small opening.

She looked down at the tray and then up to my face. Finally, she let out a barely perceptible sigh and pulled the door open just enough to accept my tray. "That's awfully nice of you, but it really wasn't necessary." Now that the door was open wider, I could see her red-rimmed eyes. She had been crying.

"Oh, I know," I told her, using as light of a tone as I could manage. "But these cinnamon buns are something else, trust me, and I really shouldn't eat them all myself."

"Well, thank you." She began to shut the door again, but I didn't want to leave her in this state.

"Have you been enjoying your stay in Crystal Cove?" It was a dumb question. Clearly she hadn't been enjoying herself, but it was all I could come up with in that instant.

Julie Miller looked behind her and then said, "The houseboat makes for a lovely place to stay."

No mention of the town. I had recently raised the prices on the houseboat rentals. When I first started managing them, I figured I'd get some quick business by offering a lower price than the local motel and bed-and-breakfasts. But that had led to me taking in some less-than-reputable tenants who had left the boats in disarray. It had been my witch friend, Marigold, who suggested that raising prices may bring in a more sophisticated clientele.

And apparently it had worked, because the Millers didn't seem like the type of couple who would leave a mess in their wake.

"Why was it you were in town?" I asked her, hoping I might get a clearer answer with her husband gone. Maybe I could offer suggestions to make her holiday a little better. While Frank gave official tours of Crystal Cove, I'd be willing to take some time the next day and show them some of the sights if she let me know what she enjoyed.

"I, um . . ." Julie looked behind her into the houseboat again. When she turned back to me, it was with a forced smile. "Just to see some family."

I was about to ask her who her family members were. I hadn't lived here long, but I'd met a lot of people through my work at the café.

But before I could get another word out, she offered one more, "Thank you," for the cinnamon buns and shut the door in my face.

Chapter Twelve

I WASN'T SURE THAT anything was off with the Millers, exactly, but something continued to bother me about them. Why were they evasive about their reasons for being in Crystal Cove? Why were they fighting? And why had they shown up on the night when another murder occurred in our town?

Then I remembered that Frank had given them an alibi for the time of the murder, so even though I'd added them to my spreadsheet, I quickly crossed their names off and kept my questions about them to myself.

But later that night, Mr. Miller appeared in my dreams. I'd kept my sea glass necklace at my bedside, in hopes it might give me some insightful dreams, but this one seemed less important and more like I was just trying to merge all of my frustrations and questions into one compact dream.

In it, John Miller was one of my customers at the café. Actually, he seemed more like a buyer than a customer. As I brewed his coffee, he kept asking me, "How much for the place?" as he surveyed the café as though he was serious.

Then Julie appeared and murmured, "Let her have it. We can't afford this."

I woke up still feeling the tension from their argument the night before. After pulling myself out of bed and trying to put them out of my mind, I had just been getting ready to walk up to The Heirloom Café for my morning coffee when a knock came at my door.

"Oh, hi!" I said when I saw it was Jay. "I was just headed out for coffee. Do you want to join me?"

Jay looked past me into the houseboat. "Actually, could we talk here for a minute?"

Ever since I'd met the detective, he was forever looking for reasons to come aboard my aunt's houseboat. Whether it had to do with my aunt's wares—most of which had already been packed away—or my insightful cat, which I still hadn't told him about fully, or about something else entirely, I wasn't sure.

"Sure. Okay." I opened the door wider. That was when I saw Mr. and Mrs. Miller heading off the wharf. Today they were hand in hand, clearly having solved any problems they'd had between them last night.

Jay came inside, and while he took a seat at the table and greeted Sherlock, I headed for the galley and my coffee maker. I didn't process well before my first cup of the day, and if we weren't going to The Heirloom, my home brew would have to do.

"Coffee?" I asked.

He shook his head. "I've already had three cups this morning. I'd better stop."

I hadn't yet dug into my cinnamon buns this morning, so I put those on a plate in the middle of the table. He didn't hesitate to help himself. It was bittersweet, knowing I wouldn't get to eat both, even though that was far more than I needed.

"To what do I owe this visit?" While Jay enjoyed coming aboard the houseboat, he had never dropped by without reason.

"Thanks," he said as he finished chewing his first bite. "Wow, this is really good!" I smiled knowingly as he chewed and swallowed and took one more bite before answering. "I talked to Mrs. Klaus, and she said some kid from the fair had come by for the bear suit early on Thursday."

"A kid? Like one of the carnies?"

Jay lifted one shoulder. "Could be. Thom's got me headed to the campground today to follow up on some inconsistencies. I wondered if you might have time to come along?"

I recalled that our local campground had been taken over by the carnies from the out-of-town carnival. Did Jay not want to go alone? Or did he think I could actually help somehow? Before I could ask, he answered my question.

"These inconsistencies have to do with which employees were at which of the carnival booths throughout the evening Thursday. I hoped with your central location at the coffee truck, you might be able to help me figure out who's not telling the truth, while I question their boss about the replaced mirror."

My eyebrows shot up. "One of them is lying to the police?" I was glad he was taking the carnival manager seriously and wondered if his employees were lying to cover for him.

Jay tilted his head and shrugged. "We're trying to figure that out. Around the time of the murder, several carnies claim to have been manning the hot dog stand, which is farthest from the Ferris wheel and I doubt they all could have been there." He pulled out a hand-drawn map of the fairgrounds and placed it on my table just as I finished fixing my coffee and sat across from him. "If they had all been here"—he pointed to a square marked with the words HOT DOG—"then that would have left these two booths unattended." He pointed to the candy stand and the one that served ice treats.

I thought back. Weren't those the carnies I had served coffee to at the beginning of the evening? I'd have to see them again to be sure.

"Sure," I told Jay. "I'd love to help." I took a bite of my cinnamon bun and was momentarily distracted. The buns were now two days old, but the dough squished in my mouth like it was fresh out of the oven. It tasted even better than it had yesterday.

I looked back to the galley. It wouldn't have been the first time something incomprehensible had happened on my aunt's houseboat, but I had to admit, if this was magic, I wasn't about to complain about it.

"Also, I talked to the parking lot attendant," Jay went on, finished with his cinnamon bun and not noticing my distraction. "He was a guy hired by the Downtown Business Association. Apparently, when Bryan Klaus took over the summer fair for this year, it was at the very last minute. The association had been running at a deficit after trying to help with local repairs after last winter's storm and they had decided months ago to cancel this year's fair. They finally made a deal to let Klaus front the money to bring in the carnival rides and booths, and once his investment was repaid, he'd offer the association ten percent of any profits over and above that. Plus the association would still get all the proceeds from the fair parking, as they always had as the originators of the summer fair."

"It seems like the association wasn't too happy about this? Could they have been angry enough to kill?"

"I haven't spoken to all of them, of course," Jay told me, "but Norm Cartwright, the parking attendant and the owner of Sensies Souvenir Shoppe in town, certainly didn't seem like he would have expected any less from Bryan Klaus. He said Klaus was a cutthroat businessman through and through, but he generally kept his word. No one liked to go up against the guy, but with enough of them to stand up for one another within the association, no one usually got railroaded too badly."

"Usually?" I asked. Everything Jay was saying certainly lined up with his mini golf employee's assessment.

He nodded. "There have been stories about people Klaus had put out of business in the past, but it seems like nothing recently. What was really interesting about my conversation with Cartwright is that he assured me there was only one way to get into the fairgrounds, and that was through him. He was also one hundred percent certain that no one had entered the fairgrounds with a large stuffed animal Thursday night. He was there from an hour before the fair opened until the last fairgoer was out of the lot that night."

"But it wasn't a stuffed bear, remember? It was only a costume."

Jay nodded. "The head of the costume was a single piece, though, and large enough that it would have been difficult to sneak in. When I showed Cartwright a photo, he assured me he hadn't seen anything like that."

"So that means the bear costume was already within the fairgrounds, or at least it had been an hour before the fair opened," I surmised.

"That's right. And where else would anyone be able to hide that size of a costume, other than in plain sight behind one of the midway booths?"

In truth, it could have also been hidden in one of the carnival's trucks, but that would still lead back to the carnival employees. It seemed like an important lead. It meant that even if the carnies or their boss hadn't killed Bryan Klaus, they were likely involved in covering it up somehow.

Before we left the boat, Jay asked in a hesitant voice, "What do you think about bringing your cat?"

It could have just been Sherlock's name that had Jay always interested in being around my cat, but I suspected it was more than that. Jay spent a lot of time looking into the supernatural aspects of cases and often used to ask my fortune-telling aunt for help. He had a feel for otherworldly things. He had even commented on the blue jewels located in the center of Sherlock's glasses and in his collar once, but that had been when I hardly knew him so I hadn't brought myself to tell him the truth.

As far as I knew, he didn't understand that these were keys to Sherlock's magical abilities, but he had commented about how similar they looked to some blue crystals that had been integral to his last case. This made me remember the blue crystal he returned, and I wondered how Rachael was doing with harnessing its powers.

As I thought about this, I absently rubbed the sea glass necklace between my thumb and forefinger. Then I blinked back to my senses, picked Sherlock up in my arms, and we headed for the door.

The local campground was about a mile down the coast and out of town. Truth be told, it wasn't much more exciting than the fairgrounds when they were empty. It was just a dusty patch of land that one of the locals had developed and added enough services to support travelers with tents and RVs. If the Oregon real estate market ever improved, the owner would be sitting on a good value, but as it was, it made sense that he didn't want to put a lot of money into it.

Today Camperland was busier than I'd ever seen it. Tents were sprawled on every available space around the perimeter of the campground, and in the center, the carnival workers had set up barbecues and picnic tables. Many of the carnies had congregated in that area.

Jay led the way toward the picnic tables, and I received a few raised eyebrows for carrying my cat along after him. I left a gap between us, so as not to take away from Jay's professionalism and authority.

As we approached, more of the carnies lingered their gazes on Jay. Several of them casually helped themselves to barbecue meat and then strayed toward tents, while others made no attempt to hide that they had no interest in talking with Jay. They took one look at him, stood, and strode away.

Jay seemed unbothered by this. I'd been learning that few things seemed to rattle him, or if they did, he didn't let it show.

"I'm looking for Mr. Carl Reitsma," he called out loud enough so even many of the stragglers near the tents would be able to hear. Carl Reitsma, Jay had explained on our way here, was the man who managed the traveling carnival.

No one reacted to this name, so he called again.

"Carl Reitsma? Are you here?" Jay turned in a circle, surveying the twenty or so guys in their teens and early twenties who were avoiding his gaze. "I just have a few questions about Thursday night, and if I can't find Mr. Reitsma, I'll have to start with all of you."

It was a smart threat. A blond boy of no more than eighteen stood from one of the picnic tables and said, "He went into town a while ago."

Jay nodded. "And where was he headed?"

The blond boy looked to the guys on either side of him, but they avoided his gaze. When he looked back to Jay, he said, "I dunno. Something about insurance?"

I got the feeling the boy was being honest. He was just trying to be helpful to his friends and get rid of the police. This felt normal for this group—self-protective and protective of one another, whether or not any of them had actually done anything wrong.

The boy looked over my shoulder, and I followed his gaze to another guy in a red baseball cap who was a little older. He shook his head at the blond boy, and when Jay pushed, asking if Mr. Reitsma had gone to visit our insurance broker in town, the boy retreated back to his seat and only said, "I can't tell you nothing else. Sorry." It felt as though he was apologizing more to the boy in the red cap than to Jay.

I glanced back to the guy behind me. I was quite certain he was the same carnie who had gotten espresso from me Thursday night. Hadn't he moved on with his espresso to man the booth with the ice treats? I'd seen Ruth buying one of those red, white, and blue frozen treats from him, I was sure of it.

I leaned in and whispered this to Jay. He made a note on his yellow, lined pad and nodded, but kept his eyes averted from the boy in the red cap.

"You've been very helpful," Jay told the blond boy, and he visibly seemed to exhale when Jay turned away from him.

"You." Jay pointed to the guy in the red cap. The bill of his cap shielded his expression, but by his suddenly tense shoulders, I could tell this young man was ready for a physical fight, if it came to that. I found myself holding my breath as Jay strode toward him and said, "I'd like you to take a walk with me."

The guy in the red cap seemed compliant enough to walk toward the perimeter of the campground with Jay. I sensed that I should leave them on their own. There weren't many people remaining near the picnic tables, and I felt as though the blond kid was eager to apologize to his friends for speaking up, but I decided not to clear out so he could do that just yet. Instead, I took a seat and felt the sea glass around my neck warm as I did.

"I guess you guys can't keep pets, being on the road and all?" I asked in an attempt to start a conversation. I ran my hand over Sherlock's fur, and he suddenly struggled to get out of my arms. "Fine, fine. You can get down for a minute. I hope no one's allergic," I said as I let him onto the bench seat beside me. "He's really friendly." Not exactly true, but one thing I knew about my newly inherited cat—he at least knew how to play a part.

Sherlock proceeded to jump onto the ground and rub up against the shins of two of the guys seated at the next table. One was the blond boy.

He reached down to pet Sherlock. Even from my place at the next table, I heard Sherlock purr in response.

So this guy seemed trustworthy—at least to my cat. I wondered how new he was to the carnival circuit and how familiar he was with the other carnies. I suspected if Jay could get him alone, we might get some clearer answers about the different carnies' whereabouts on Thursday evening.

"He likes you," I told the boy. "Don't you, Sherlock?"

The boy's eyebrow shot up. "Your cat's name is Sherlock?" He picked up my cat, and I had the distinct impression from how comfortably he did it that he was used to being friendly with small animals.

"That's right," I told him. "He was actually my aunt's cat, but he got passed down to me after my aunt died. We're still getting to know each other, aren't we, Sherlock?"

My cat didn't look in my direction, but the boy had met my cat's eyes and this seemed to be earning trust from both of them.

Not so much from the boy's friends, though. They got up and one of them said, "You'd better come back to the tent soon," to him as they moved away.

The boy nibbled his lip, taking in their instruction, but didn't respond.

"Do you have any pets back at home?" I toyed with my sea glass and kept the topic on pets in an attempt to keep him here on his own. It seemed to be working, at least for the moment. "You sure seem good with him."

The boy nodded, looking even younger than he had only a minute ago. "I really miss my cat, Mistral."

When I was in middle school, several of my schoolmates used to joke about running away with the circus. I suddenly wondered if this idea wasn't such a joke. Surely this youngster, who I now thought was closer to fifteen than eighteen, wasn't traveling with the carnival with his parents' permission.

"How often do you get to go home and see Mistral? I'll bet this carnival keeps you pretty busy." The boy stiffened at my question, but Sherlock responded by purring even louder and rubbing up against his chin. It seemed to calm him.

"Not in a while." His words were short and quiet. My sea glass cooled in my fingers and I got the sense that if I kept following up on questions about his home life, he'd soon disappear to the tents with his coworkers.

"Do you run one of the rides with the carnival?" I prattled on before he could actually answer, trying to get him to let his guard down and think of me as an interested tourist. "Whenever I see those rides go up so quickly, in less than a day, it amazes me. You guys must have worked out a real system."

The boy nodded, his attention more on Sherlock, who lapped up his affection, than on me. "They have a system, yeah, but I just run the hot dog stand. It's a pretty easy setup."

The hot dog stand? Wasn't that the stand that several of the carnies had claimed to be working at while a murder took place? I suddenly wondered if this was just a standard answer they'd all been ordered to give if they ever got questioned by the police. "Oh yeah? Do you ever make cotton candy or those caramel apples? I love those."

"Nah. I'm pretty new, so they haven't taught me all that yet, but Carl says soon I can learn the ice cream booth and then

I'll be able to switch it up through the days and not just be stuck on hot dogs."

"Is ice cream really a step up from hot dogs?" Was there some sort of hierarchy to the carnival jobs, and if so, could that help us nail down who, exactly, could have been moving stuffed animals from booth to booth throughout the evening and who would have definitely stayed put?

The boy shrugged. "Ice cream's finicky. It has to be kept at the right temperature through the heat in the day and the cool evenings, and the cooler isn't very reliable. I know I could handle it, but it's just about where Carl wants to put us."

I was about to clarify that this Carl, the carnival manager, knew everyone's stations throughout Thursday night, but I caught myself before I said something that might threaten this kid and make him run. Instead, I held out a hand. "I'm Tabby, by the way. I live on my aunt's houseboat at the local marina and work at the local coffee shop in town. I was running the coffee truck at the fair until the whole thing got shut down." I hoped my words would make him feel as though I was as much a bystander in this as he seemed to be.

"Grady." The one word was all he gave me, and he didn't shake my hand.

"I was surprised at how busy the food booths were. You'd think everyone would rush for the rides, but apparently everyone needed coffee first." I laughed. "My boss thought I'd be able to handle the coffee truck all on my own, but really there should have been two of us."

Grady chuckled, too, and I was glad to see him relaxing. "Yeah, we need two people at most of our booths, but Carl says people can wait. He'll only hire enough for one at each booth."

I shook my head. "I guess that's the part that's not down to a system yet, huh?" I didn't leave time for an answer. "Only one ride operator per ride, too, or does he at least allow for more help there?"

Grady shook his head, looking like he'd talked about this injustice plenty of times with his coworkers. "One per ride, plus one floater, in case there's an emergency or someone has to go to the bathroom."

"At least that's something," I conceded. "But it probably leaves a lot of burden on you guys if this floater isn't around, huh?"

He nodded in agreement. Sherlock kneaded his lap, keeping Grady at least half distracted and at ease.

"But I guess the floater knows how to run everything, right? So he can take over any booth or ride quickly?"

"After all these years, Ian better know how to run everything." Grady dropped his voice to almost a whisper, but there was a definite edge to it. I was just glad to have a name. "If you ask me, Carl should teach someone else to run all the rides. Ian's lazy as anything, and half the time when we need him, he's off vaping behind one of the trucks."

I raised my eyebrows. "Not much work ethic, huh?"

"And then he makes us look bad when anything goes wrong. But he's been with

Carl for years, so I doubt anything's going to change."

"Does he give you a hassle when you call him for help at the hot dog stand?" I asked.

Grady let out a humorless chuckle. "Wouldn't know. Haven't ever asked, since he tells Carl anyone who needs his help is incompetent."

"So you never even need him to relieve you for the bathroom?"

Grady shook his head, aligning his shoulders and looking proud at this fact. "Nope. Never asked for help once. I think that's why Carl's moving me up to another booth so quickly. He put the other new guy on ice cream because he's five years older, but I think he's going to switch us. The guy is constantly calling for Ian or sometimes even leaving his booth completely unattended. I'm pretty sure he'll be on hot dogs soon and I'll get the ice cream and maybe even candy soon enough."

I was about to ask who this incompetent ice cream worker was.

If he confirmed it was the guy in the red cap, and if that carnie often couldn't be accounted for, we might have something. I just needed a name. But just then, Jay reappeared, and as he strode toward us, it seemed to knock the severity of the situation back into Grady.

He held Sherlock out toward me. "I should go."

I nodded and took my cat. As it was, I could probably come back and question Grady some more if I needed to, but I had a feeling that if Jay the detective got involved, Grady may never be seen outside his tent again.

Chapter Thirteen

Jay and I were in his unmarked police car before either of us talked about what we had discovered.

"Did that kid have anything interesting to say?" he asked.

"I'm not sure if any of it was important." The more I'd been thinking about it, this young kid, Grady, may have only been trying to keep me busy. What if he was the low man on the totem pole, assigned to keep strangers occupied whenever they came poking around? He had, after all, stood up upon our arrival and been the only one to speak.

Nevertheless, I went on to explain the hierarchy among carnies that he'd told me about.

"But he claims to have worked at the hot dog stand?" Jay sighed, and this seemed to punctuate the fact that I'd just been played. But then he asked something that I'd forgotten about. "Did Sherlock trust him?"

I thought back to how Sherlock had been purring on his lap and snuggling up to him. After a while, it hadn't seemed like a ploy to get a suspect talking, but rather like Sherlock and Grady were actually filling a need in each other—in long-separated owner and cat.

"Sherlock loved Grady," I told Jay. This type of question would never be broached by Aaron, and he certainly wouldn't put any stock in my cat's reaction. It was nice to be able to share these details with Jay. Hopefully, once I got Sherlock alone, I'd come up with even more information to bring back to Jay. "So, yeah, that might say something."

Jay nodded. "As soon as he volunteered to speak to me when we arrived, I got the sense he was new to this business. Just a young kid who generally told the truth."

"You don't think he could have been the fall guy for the other employees? You know, low man on the totem pole talks to the police kind of thing?"

"I didn't get that impression." Jay's words relieved me. I liked Grady. He seemed like a good kid. "And Kevin Marshall, the carnie I was speaking to? I asked him to weigh in on the kid who had spoken up. He said Grady hadn't even been around a month and didn't know what he was talking about. It felt like there was some animosity there."

"Kevin, that's the carnie in the red baseball cap, right?"

"That's right. I asked him how long he'd been with the carnival, and he didn't seem to want to admit that he hadn't been around much longer than Grady."

I explained what Grady had told me about Ian, the longest-employed carnie who was the floater and could run any of the booths and rides. I also relayed how Grady had told me the other new carnie, the one in the red baseball cap, was on ice cream. "He bought a coffee from me at the beginning of the evening," I told Jay. "Then he and his friends dispersed to their booths. I'm quite sure I had seen the carnie in the red had at the ice cream booth myself."

"Did seeing the employees jog any other memories of where others had been working?" Jay asked.

"I couldn't be sure with the others, but seeing the kid in the red cap again—it made me remember later in the evening when he'd served Ruth and her friends those red, blue, and white popsicles."

"And you're sure it was him?"

I nodded. "Pretty sure. Yeah."

"Well, that's interesting, because he told me he was working the hot dog stand Thursday night."

I nibbled my lip. "The whole night? I can't be sure he was at the ice treats all night. Just at the beginning and when Ruth arrived. But Grady insisted he didn't leave the hot dog stand even once and that there was only one carnie working at each booth."

Jay shook his head as we arrived back at the marina. "Kevin also said he was serving hot dogs all night without a break."

"It seems like if you find the floater, the carnie who was moving around all night, he might have a good idea of who was where and who could have left their stations." I was still convinced that Grady had been working the hot dog stand and this Kevin guy was on ice treats. But why would anyone lie about this?

It brought me back to the fact that somehow one or both of them were trying to cover for their boss.

"I plan to look into that," Jay told me. "But for the moment, if what Kevin tells me is correct, I should be able to connect with Carl Reitsma, the manager of the carnival, down at our local insurance office. Apparently, he's been given the runaround about getting reimbursed for having to shut the carnival down, so he planned to gain some ammunition from someone who understood policy language."

I wasn't sure whether or not I was glad this Carl Reitsma had insurance. I wouldn't wish for anyone's business to be suddenly shut down due to a murder, but I also had a strange feeling that all these half-truths among carnies trickled down from the top.

Chapter Fourteen

JAY FELT IT WAS safest to take another officer with him to confront Carl Reitsma instead of me, but I couldn't seem to sit still at the houseboat. It didn't take long before I came up with another angle I could look into myself.

I'd been to Marigold Weather's house one time before. While I'd thought of my aunt's houseboat as having been the ultimate expression of magical housing, it paled in comparison to Marigold's small house. Every inch of her fortune-telling central held a magic wand or a dreamcatcher or a leather-bound book of spells.

My aunt had been the most renowned fortune-teller in town when she'd been alive, while Marigold had worked with what she called a "variety of the magical arts," but since my aunt had left a large clientele of locals who liked to regularly have their fortunes read, Marigold spent most of her time telling fortunes these days.

I had never been into the upstairs of the house where Marigold lived, as her fortune-telling clients and her visitors always went around through the back garden, led by signs boasting "THIS WAY TO YOUR FUTURE . . ."

But today I hadn't called ahead, and I didn't want to interrupt if she was currently with a client, so I headed up the three front cement steps to a very normal-looking navy front door.

I knocked, and while I waited, I pulled out my phone, wondering if I should try calling. Dropping by unannounced had seemed like a good idea a few minutes ago, but for all I knew, Marigold was working at her son's grocery mart today, which she did a few days per week.

I sighed and knocked again, already having pretty much given up on my great idea of following up on the witch's boycotting signs while Jay was busy with Carl Reitsma. But then a curtain moved in the front window. I was sure of it.

I knocked again, louder this time. The door still didn't open to me; however, I knew I'd seen the curtain move. I had no idea if Marigold lived alone, but she was too old to have young children, so there was no reason not to open the door to me.

Unless she was hiding something.

I lifted my hand to knock again, but that was when her door flew open. Marigold stood on the other side, her normally poufy purple hair flat against her head. She wore a gray sweat suit, which made her look her sixtysomething age, even with the bright purple hair.

"What is it, Tabitha?" Most of the local witches had warmed to me, apparent in them casually calling me Tabby. While

I'd always thought Marigold liked me more than most new-to-towners, it was her natural reflex to keep people at a distance. That was clearer in this moment than it ever had been.

"I, um, I just wanted to talk to you about Bryan Klaus."

She pulled back. "Klaus? Why on earth do you want to talk about him?"

I motioned to her door. She was blocking the view of the inside of her house, but I wasn't going to be deterred. "Can I just come in for a minute?"

Her forehead buckled, but after a pause, she relented. "I'll meet you downstairs."

Before she closed the door, I got a small glimpse of her upper living space. It was surprisingly average, with a couch and a loveseat in shades of beige, and the artwork hung on the walls looked like something that could have decorated a hotel room. This, from the place that Marigold Weathers spent her days, was more than surprising.

When her door shut in my face, I retraced my steps down the front path and then around through her garden. It was several minutes later when a deadbolt let out a loud clack and her basement door opened.

To say she looked different than a few minutes ago was an understatement. In the short time she'd taken to meet me downstairs, she'd thrown on a floor-length orange dress and pouffed her purple hair into a messy bouffant.

Her smile was new, too, covered in red lipstick and obviously put on. "Tabitha! Do come in." She swung her basement door open as though she were a game show hostess.

I walked through, taking in the magic-infused space. It appeared the same as the last time I'd been here, covered in magic memorabilia. "I don't want to take up much of your time. You don't have clients today?"

This question seemed to annoy her. The other witches had told me many times that Marigold liked to pretend she was swamped with customers, even when in reality she kept a second job at her son's grocery mart to pay her bills, so I immediately realized my mistake.

"I mean, I'm sure you have some later, but I just wanted to ask you about your thoughts on what happened to Bryan Klaus on Thursday."

"Bryan . . . Klaus?" she asked, as though she may not even recognize his name. In a town the size of Crystal Cove, that would have been impossible to believe.

"Yes, the fair manager? Who was found dead on the Ferris wheel?"

Finally, she nodded and sighed. She took a seat at her small round table in the center of the room and offered me the chair opposite from her. "Oh, yes, of course. Just awful what happened there." Her lip twitched as though she was holding back a smile. It wouldn't have surprised me. The witches around Crystal Cover were all known to hold grudges, but none more than Marigold.

"Last I heard, you were in charge of boycotting the fair because of Mr. Klaus?" I asked it as a question.

She glanced toward the door. "Are you here on some sort of official business?" She knew I'd gotten to know Jay and Aaron since moving to town.

But this, at least, I could answer honestly. "Not officially, no. I just wanted to follow up on my own questions."

She nodded. "Well, you have it wrong. I made some signage and put it up before the fair started, but if you really want to know who was in charge of boycotting this year's fair, you'd be best to talk to Sheena Park."

"Sheena? But she was at the fair?"

Marigold raised her eyebrows, as though waiting for me to catch up.

"Did she plan to do something to get back at Mr. Klaus during the fair?"

Now Marigold let the smile work fully onto her face. "I couldn't say for sure, of course. But we all heard about her plans of making sure word got around by Friday that people shouldn't bother attending this year."

I thought back to seeing Sheena Thursday night. She had pretty much flown under my radar. Certain witches in town did that—they seemed to move in and around town without anyone noticing them. These witches seemed possibly more dangerous than the loud and boisterous ones like Marigold. I'd been keeping my eye on Ruth, for instance, as her quiet demeanor always kept me on my guard around her. But I guess I'd been so busy watching Rachael and Ruth at the fair, I'd barely noticed Sheena.

"What did Sheena plan to do Thursday?" I leaned forward across the table, in case Marigold only wanted to whisper the answer.

But as usual, she was happy to say what she had to contribute loud and proud. "Well, she planned to upset the cart in any way she could, of course." Marigold studied her nails. "Now that Klaus is dead, she won't admit to much, but I happen to know she manipulated some of their electrical wiring and made a mess of their fun house."

"Their fun house?" I sucked in a breath. "How? What did she do to it?"

Marigold shrugged. "I think she just dumped some soda and sticky candy in the mirror maze. Whatever it took to shut it down for the night." Marigold's voice had gotten quieter, like she wasn't willing to give any kind of kudos to another witch in town, even though part of her was impressed.

But as far as I was concerned, I was likely interviewing the wrong witch. "Thanks for telling me. I'm glad to know you weren't around at the time of Mr. Klaus's death."

She tilted her head and shrugged, which I wondered if it meant she would have actually loved to have been there.

I got up and apologized again for stopping by unannounced.

"Are you going to do the same thing to Sheena?" Again, it was hard to tell if this idea made Marigold feel elated or protective of her on-again, off-again witch friend.

"Well, I do want to talk to her." And I know where she lives, I thought but didn't say. If I seemed too eager, I had no doubt Marigold would stick her nose into the situation and forewarn Sheena before I could connect with Jay and then get to her apartment. So I added my own shrug, in hopes it would help her leave the situation alone. "I'm not as close to Sheena, so I'll probably have to call first."

This was enough to get Marigold to relax about the whole thing. Whether or not she actually believed we were close, it put her mind at ease to believe I thought so.

Even if I was only using my acting ability.

When I returned to the Lady of Fortune, I walked in, took one look around, and momentarily thought I'd been robbed. Detective novels were everywhere, covering almost every inch of the main floor, most of them splayed open.

I looked at Sherlock in the middle of the mess as he methodically flipped pages in one, ignoring my entrance. "Did you do all this?" I motioned around the floor. "Are you even strong enough to pull the books off the shelf by yourself?" As I asked the question, I had to wonder if my aunt's houseboat, which had given me more than one indication that it had magical powers of its own, had at least helped.

I picked up a couple of novels and stacked them to make a path as I entered. I had almost made it to Sherlock when my phone pinged with a new text. MOM came up on the screen, and in that instant, I knew exactly what it was about. I clicked on it.

~Did you have a chance to talk to Pepper?~

I slapped my forehead. With all the craziness since Thursday night, I'd completely forgotten to call my sister. Rather than replying to my mom, I navigated to Pepper's number and hit dial.

With all Mom had gone on about how difficult Pepper was to reach, I expected her voice mail. I was surprised when she picked up.

"Tabby? Hi!" She sounded genuinely happy to hear from me. Another surprise.

"Hey, Dr. Pepper." It was what I had called her since the day she'd been accepted into medical school. "Mom says she's been trying to get a hold of you."

This seemed to somber her. "Oh. Yeah. Can you just tell her everything's fine but I'm just really busy getting ready for midterms?"

I could. But for some reason, I had the sense that everything wasn't fine. I toyed with the sea glass around my neck, and it warmed between my fingers. "Are you sure everything's all right? You sound stressed."

My baby sister was nothing if not easy to read. She'd always worn her emotions on her sleeves. Her long sigh didn't hide anything.

"Come on, Pepps. What is it?"

Another sigh. "You can't tell Mom and Dad . . ."

"I don't know if I've mentioned, but Dad is not speaking to me." I had mentioned this several times since moving to Crystal Cove. Each time I did, Pepper had treated the situation with a strange kind of respect, like she wished she could do something that would rile up our dad that much. "And Mom just really wants to know you're okay. So what's the truth? Are you really okay?"

She groaned. "I'm failing." Before I could respond, she added, "That might be hopeful thinking. I'm pretty sure I've already failed."

I shook my head, thinking of how our dad had pushed her to barrel ahead with a summer semester, rather than taking a break for a few months. Dad was like that—go, go, go and deal with the consequences later. Our brother was a bit like that, too, but this was the first time it had occurred to me that Pepper might be more like me: the type who needed to step back and reassess once in a while. Maybe even change course.

Although, that wasn't true either. All Pepper had wanted since high school was to become a research physician. She'd worked hard every step of the way, always headed in the same direction. Not like me, who'd already tried out a dozen careers. I still wasn't exactly sure what I was meant to do with my life, but my Crystal Cove pursuits felt righter than anything I'd done in the past. At this thought, my sea glass grew even warmer.

"You should have taken the summer off, like Mom and I suggested," I told her. My sea glass instantly grew cold, and I immediately wanted to slap myself. What she didn't need right now was a lecture. "I'm sorry, Pepps. Is there any way to get through this semester? Then you could always take a break in the fall. Come back fresh for the winter session?"

Another sigh. "I need a break now. I thought about coming for a visit. It seems like Crystal Cove has helped you get your head on straight. Maybe it's being near the ocean . . ."

"Seattle's near the ocean" popped out as an automatic response. She was currently studying at the University of Washington's School of Medicine, which was only a few miles from the nearest beach. But my argument wasn't really about that.

She knew it, too. "You don't want me to come." It wasn't a question.

"It's not that. I just . . . Dad's already so angry with me, and if he all of a sudden found out you'd left school in the middle of a semester to come and visit me?"

That was only part of the reason. The other part, if I was being honest with myself, was that I was finally finding a bit of footing in what I was meant to do. Plus, I felt like I could be an honest help to my detective friends in town, doing something important. Besides that, no one in my family would be ready to hear about a magical cat or a supernatural houseboat, even my sister.

Before Pepper could respond, I added, "It's not like you to run away from your problems."

Pepper let out a humorless laugh, but I knew her well enough to hear the drive behind it. One thing she'd never been accused of was being a coward. "You're right," she said eventually. "I'm not going to run away. I'll at least stick out this semester."

I felt bad at her possibly still feeling jilted, so I said, "But after the semester, you should definitely take a break and come and visit. You can meet Aunt Lizzie's cat. He's very smart." It wasn't enough truth to make my sea glass warm, but at least it was no longer ice cold in my hand.

"A cat?" I could hear the distaste in my sister's voice, but I was pretty sure she'd warm up to Sherlock, too, once she got to know him.

And now I had a goal: to get my life sorted out before September so I could truly be happy to have Pepper come for a visit.

After hanging up, I sent a quick text to our mom, letting her know that Pepper was in the middle of midterms and didn't have time to chat, but she was otherwise fine and taking care of herself. I'd just hit send when a knock sounded at my door.

"Come on in," I said, hoping it was Jay stopping by to let me know what he'd discovered from Carl Reitsma. Instead, the door opened to reveal my renter from next door.

John Miller looked around the interior of my houseboat with his brow furrowed. The houseboat he was renting next door was much larger and more modern. It had an open layout similar to a house. Mine definitely looked like a small boat—inside and out. Finally, his gaze landed on me and Sherlock, surrounded by books. His face morphed into a smile, but it still held a hint of confusion behind it.

I had no way to explain this, so I didn't even try. I pushed to a standing position. "What can I help you with, Mr. Miller?"

He cleared his throat loudly. "I just wanted to let you know Julie and I are clearing out a day early."

My eyebrows shot up. "You're leaving today? Is something wrong with the houseboat?"

He shook his head. "Have to get back on business. I don't suppose you can rebate me for the night." Before I could answer, he added, "I'm sure it would be a pain to figure it out with the credit card bill, so how about you just charge me the full amount on the card and you can give me some cash to make up the difference?"

It was too late to rebook the houseboat for tonight, and I'd already covered the cost of his first night. If I'd known ahead of time, I might have been able to rebook it, as I had two new sets of renters coming into other houseboats tonight, and the one the Millers were occupying was usually the favorite. But I'd also promised Rachael the cleaning job for all the boats, and this didn't give her much notice.

"I don't think so," I told him honestly. I was on the hook for the money to the houseboat owner, after all.

His smile flattened. It was the first time I'd seen him lose what I'd subconsciously thought of as his politician's smile. "Should have known," he muttered and turned on his heel as though this was my fault, letting my door slam shut. The boat rocked as he strode off it, and I stood there stunned with my mouth open.

What a jerk! But at the same time, my house rental business was a new one. I wasn't a pushover, but it was a delicate situation with a new business and I was willing to look for a compromise. I hadn't had a single unhappy customer so far, and I really didn't want to start with Mr. Miller going online and leaving a scathing Yelp review. Maybe I could offer him and his wife a deal if they chose to come back later in the summer.

I popped to my feet to go and suggest this, but by the time I got out my door and under the purple curtains, John Miller had already disappeared into the houseboat next door. Julie Miller stood out on the front deck, looking up toward the main road. I followed her gaze to where I saw a flash of red moving away from the marina and then disappearing behind a tree.

Was that a red baseball cap?

I wasn't crazy enough to think that just because I'd seen a flash of a red hat, this was the same carnie Jay had been questioning earlier today.

But what if it was?

I ducked out from under the purple curtains just as Julie Miller headed back inside her houseboat. I raced across the gangplank, down the wharf, and took a leap off the last stair onto the shore. Seconds later, I was up the embankment and behind the tree where I'd see the red hat disappear.

He was no longer there, but I could swear I saw another flash of red beyond the truck stop that led south to the coastal highway and out of town.

That route also led to our local campground.

I picked up to a jog, becoming more convinced that the flash of red was the carnie who had been evasive with Jay earlier. Traffic was always busy in the downtown core of Crystal Cove during the summer, often with tourists passing through for the day to visit one of our many souvenir shops, and I had to stop and wait to cross the road. As soon as I found an opening, I jogged south after where I'd seen the red hat disappear.

As I moved out of the main area of town and finally made it to the highway, there were plenty of red vehicles in sight, but not another single person on foot. Which made sense. Who would choose to walk along the highway outside of town?

I must have been mistaken about the guy's route. While I'd waited to cross the street, he must have turned along Second Street, staying within the town center. I'd been so convinced it had been the same carnie and that he'd been headed back toward the campground that I hadn't considered the most realistic option: any person on foot was much more likely to have wandered back up Second Street, rather than out to the highway.

I sighed at myself and headed back toward town. I walked up Second Street and back down Main, but there was no sign of anyone in a red hat. My sea glass grew cold around my neck, and I figured my investigative sense was probably just overreaching from all the detective novels I'd been reading to Sherlock.

As I arrived back at the marina, I passed the Millers' white sedan in the parking lot, and the license plate caught my eye. It was from Washington, although they'd never told me where they'd come from. The first three letters of their license plate spelled out JOY. I had to chuckle, thinking of John Miller and his politician's smile, and then I imagined my dad with a similar license plate. I thought the O might actually be a zero, but still, it struck me as humorous that this man was labeled joyful everywhere he went.

It was later that day when the Millers had cleared out and I arranged for

Rachael to clean the rental houseboat for a family that would be arriving the following day. I had wanted to get her alone so I could ask her a few pointed questions about Sheena's dislike of Bryan Klaus, but as I let her in, I gave the place a once-over and my mouth dropped open. Given the Miller's neat appearance, I never would have expected such a mess. The galley was a pigsty—like they hadn't turned on the dishwasher or even thought about scraping their plates through their entire stay. It smelled like old fish, and I crossed the open space to crack open the largest window, immediately regretting that I'd let them book without a deposit. Both bedrooms were also messy. Either they just wanted to make an extra hassle for us or the couple didn't sleep together. Honestly, at this point, either option would not have surprised me, and I was extra glad I hadn't given them a cash refund.

"I'm sorry," I told Rachael. "I'll pay you extra for this one."

She shrugged as if she'd seen worse. "Any new information from Detective Thom on what happened to Bryan Klaus?" She knew I was friendly with two detectives on the force, but she usually avoided the topic of me talking to Jay.

I was glad she brought it up, but I had to tread carefully. "I think there are some inconsistencies from the carnival employees." Jay often trusted me with more information than he should, so I left it vague. "Speaking of Bryan Klaus, I hear your friend Sheena really didn't like the guy?"

Rachael looked out the window, pensive for a moment, and then answered my question with one of her own. "No other suspects besides the carnival employees?" She started unpacking her cleaning supplies, but I had the distinct impression she was avoiding my eyes. I wondered if Marigold had already put out a warning through the witch circles about me poking around with questions.

But before I could press her further, she reached into her pocket and, a second later, held out my blue crystal in her open hand. "I tried a couple of spells, but again, they went horribly wrong. I almost caught my apartment on fire this morning. I don't think I'm ready for it." She moved it a few inches in my direction.

I resisted taking a step away, but finally reached out and took it, and immediately felt that overwhelmed sensation again. My mind went hazy to everything around me, and all I seemed to be able to think about was the crystal. I clearly wasn't ready for its magical powers either, but how could I force them back on her?

I was in such a sudden haze, I barely heard her when she said, "I'll let you know when I'm done."

I arrived back at the Lady of Fortune-, barely remembering getting myself there. Using all of my mental strength, I moved toward the front cockpit—an area I rarely ventured into—and I placed the blue crystal that was still in the baggie into the glovebox.

I took in a deep breath and let it out on a sigh, already able to think more clearly. As I made my way back into the main cabin, my mind became clearer yet, and I realized maybe Rachael wasn't acting strange or evasive due to the investigation around Bryan Klaus. Maybe it had only been the effects of the crystal.

For the moment, I tried to put the crystal out of my mind. If I had to, I'd return it to Jay, but perhaps stowing it out of reach until I could learn more about its powers would be enough. It had belonged to my aunt, after all, so I didn't want to get rid of it if I could help it.

Focusing on real-world tasks to help balance my mind, I pulled up my payment app to process the Millers' credit card. Everything in me wanted to charge an extra damage deposit amount on top of their rate for the mess they'd left, but I forced a couple of deep breaths and hit process with the regular rental rate I'd quoted them.

I waited as the circle turned in the middle of my phone, letting me know it was working. I was ready to put their stay behind me, glad I hadn't comped them another free night. My phone buzzed in my hand when it finished processing. I looked down at my screen but didn't see the confirmation I was expecting.

STOLEN CARD.

This was followed by a phone number I was supposed to call to report it, as well as instructions to keep the credit card. I, of course, did not have John Miller's actual card, but I navigated to my phone app to call the credit card company.

After giving my report, the lady on the other end gave me an earful about not taking a deposit. Again, I felt like an inexperienced idiot for trusting people so easily. Was I even cut out for running my own business? What if my dad was right about me and I should just go back to being someone's realtor employee, no matter how they treated me?

I was on the phone for fifteen minutes, repeating the same small amount of information several times to three different people before they finally let me go.

I'd still have to pay the houseboat owner, but now it looked like it would come out of my own pocket. It didn't sound like I was going to get a dime out of John and Julie Miller, or whoever they were.

Chapter Fifteen

I HAD JUST HUNG up when a knock sounded at my door. I wondered what Rachael had forgotten and swung open my door, already speaking. "What do you need?"

But it was Jay. He furrowed his brow at me as his smile flattened.

"Oh. Sorry. I thought you were Rachael." My frustration was evident in my voice.

"Can I come in for a minute?" Unfortunately, it was awkward to let him aboard today. Besides the fact that I wasn't going to be good company at the moment, I still had detective novels splayed open all over the floor. I also felt bad letting him inside while Rachael was right next door. Rachael had an unrelenting crush on the guy, and the last thing I needed was for her to see him hanging out at my place when he didn't usually give her the time of day.

Then again, the longer he stood outside my door, the more I chanced her seeing him here, even with the purple curtains. I knew for a fact that Rachael always liked to start with the bathrooms and then bedrooms when she cleaned—getting the worst parts over with first, she always said—and so I figured if I had a short window to let Jay inside and find out what he wanted, it was probably now.

"Sure, come on in." Even though I had plenty to relay to him, I automatically asked, "What's up?"

As usual, he surveyed the inside of the houseboat thoroughly before saying any more. I picked up a few more detective novels and slid them back on the bookshelf as he made his way across the small space. He looked at the empty table, the hand-drawn and hand-woven art on the walls, the pencil-drawn sketch of Crystal Cove, and finally at Sherlock, now curled up on the loveseat napping.

He headed straight for my cat and took a seat beside him. He ran a hand over Sherlock's fur, and Sherlock shifted but didn't obviously wake up. I knew that cat well enough by this point to know he was only faking sleep. I got so few visitors, he would be paying special attention when one arrived, especially knowing this particular visitor might have some clues to an investigation.

"You seem upset," he said, stating the obvious.

I let out a humorless laugh. "Yeah, my latest renters stiffed me using a stolen credit card."

He raised his eyebrows, half standing. "Are they still here? I'll go talk to them."

I shook my head. "They left a couple of hours ago."

Jay pulled out a notepad and pen. "What information do you have on them? I'll see what I can find out about tracking them down."

I tilted my head. "That's super nice of you, but basically all I have are their names, which I now realize were probably fake, and the stolen card number. Which I already reported, by the way."

"Good, good." He nodded and sat back down. "But what did they look like? Where did they say they were from? What were they driving?"

Leave it to Jay to be much better at detective work than I was. I hadn't considered that there might actually be some way to catch these people. I gave him the best description I could and that they came from Washington, as far as I could tell by their car. I even mentioned the "JOY-ful" license plate.

"White sedan, huh?" He made a note. "Could be a rental."

Which would make them that much harder to find.

"Don't give up hope," he said, as though he could read my mind. "I'll let you know what I figure out."

After he'd been so ready to help me, I wanted to return the favor. "While you were busy with the case, I dropped by to see Marigold Weathers." I had his full attention, and he even poised his pen, ready to take more notes. "She seemed to think Sheena Park was the angriest of all the witches about Bryan Klaus's shunning of them, and apparently putting up signs was not enough for her." I explained how Marigold thought she had planned to attend the fair to do what she could to interfere with their rides and electrical wiring. "And apparently, she had planned to dump soda and sticky candy throughout the fun house."

Jay stopped writing and looked at me with raised eyebrows. "Did you question Sheena?"

I shook my head. "I figured I should wait for you."

I thought about telling him that I'd started to ask Rachael about it, who was next door at this very minute, but I didn't really want him to barrel over there and interrogate her about her friend, and I didn't want to admit that I hadn't been able to ask her a single useful question on my own.

He nodded and continued writing. "Probably a good idea. But the reason I came by was because your friend Grady dropped by the station this afternoon," he finally said.

Grady was far from being my friend, but that would be arguing semantics. "What did he want?"

"Well, I thought I'd cleared his boss, Carl Reitsma, from suspicion. Reitsma showed me where he had replaced a piece of mirror Thursday, and it wasn't even in the fun house. It was on the carousel, and it even showed signs of dust where it had been cut and mounted." Jay looked from Sherlock to me and raised an eyebrow. "I thought I'd cleared all of the carnival workers from suspicion, but then Grady walked into the station to tell me he'd been lying to you about being stationed at the hot dog stand the other night. He'd actually been selling ice treats, or so he says."

"You don't believe him?" I didn't either. I'd seen the guy in the red cap, Kevin, selling an ice treat to Ruth and her friends. I thought again about mentioning the possibility of seeing the guy with the red baseball cap here at the marina, and as I thought that, another idea dawned on me. What if Kevin had come by to talk to me, to try and convince me that Grady was lying, but Mrs. Miller had come outside right then and scared him off?

My heart beat a little faster at the thought of one of the carnies purposely tracking me down here at my boat. I had told Grady this was where I lived, after all. And why did they all seem to be lying about their whereabouts that night?

Jay shook his head. "The guy was sweating something awful, despite the air conditioning in the station, and his breathing seemed labored. All signs of lying."

"So do you think the other carnies threatened him and made him go in and confess a lie to the police?" Before Jay could answer, I threw out a few of my other questions. "There's obviously some lying or covering up going on among the carnies. What are they covering up? Could one of the carnies have truly killed Mr. Klaus? But they were only in town for a few days, so if so, what was their motive? And why are the others trying to cover it up, unless it's either for their boss or a long-term worker who they're all friends with?" Jay opened his mouth, but I wasn't done yet. "Or maybe several of them were in on it together. Maybe Carl Reitsma and his floater, Ian?" I thought again about the passage in the detective novel about a family working together and wondered if any of the carnies had the last name Reitsma.

Jay nodded, raising both his eyebrows, probably to check if I was done. When I didn't immediately say any more, he started to offer his thoughts. "Any combination of them certainly could be responsible, but I haven't figured out a motive. When I had Carl Reitsma show me the replaced mirror at the fairgrounds, he corroborated Kevin's account. Apparently, he'd recently trained Grady on the icy treats booth because he'd proven himself competent. He said he has no idea why the young kid would lie and said he'd been at the hot dog stand—unless he was just afraid of the police."

My sea glass warmed. I gripped it and shook my head as my confidence about this solidified. "No, it was definitely the guy in the red hat at the icy treats booth. I saw him with my own eyes. I'm also fairly sure Grady wasn't lying to me when he said he was working at the hot dog booth Thursday. As far as he knew, we were just having a conversation. I got the feeling he's a runaway, though, so he definitely has some secrets."

Jay nodded. "Yeah, I talked his family details out of him. He sweated a little harder over that subject, but when I told him I wasn't investigating a runaway at the moment, only a murder, and if he didn't kill anybody, he didn't have anything to worry about, he came clean about his family. I got a hold of them, and he wasn't lying, at least about that part. Sadly, it didn't seem like they were in any hurry for him to return home."

Even though I'd just met the young guy, I felt bad for him. As much as I didn't see eye to eye with any of my family, at least I felt as though I was wanted.

The thought of family brought this question back to me. "You have all the names of the carnival employees, right? Do any of them have the last name Reitsma?"

Jay raised his eyebrows. "No. Why would you think one of them is related to their boss?"

I didn't know how to explain the fact that my cat had suggested it by choosing and reading a specific detective novel, so I just told him, "It was just a thought."

"And you were right about the fun house." As soon as Jay said the words,

Sherlock poked his head up and looked right at him, as if he somehow knew this was going to be the most important clue. "Even though the replaced mirror hadn't come from there, we found traces of blood that hadn't been wiped up very well in the mirror maze of the fun house. We're waiting for a DNA match, but it matches the blood type of Bryan Klaus. We'll be looking a lot closer at the carnie who was running the fun house Thursday night."

"The guy with the blue hair?" I had already told Jay how I'd spoken to him on my way to the rides that night but hadn't seen him at the campground. I tried to put all of these pieces together in my head. Could the blue-haired carnie have broken a shard of mirror from the carousel and taken it to the fun house with him? Then again, Mr. Reitsma had replaced the mirror earlier in the day. I wondered where the old mirror had gone.

"That's right," Jay said, taking my attention. "But none of the carnies I've talked to were sporting a blue streak, so I suspect either this guy's hiding from me or he's recently given himself a dye job."

I wasn't sure why Jay had told me so much about the case until he said, "Listen, Tabby. I realize it's not my place to ask, but our force is severely understaffed, and if I send Thom to the campground, I have no doubt the secrecy and lies are only going to increase." He gave me a hint of a smile, enough to bring on his dimples.

But I wasn't sure what he was asking. "What do you want me to do?"

He instantly went serious again. "You were able to make Grady feel at ease and get more of a clear sense from him than we could. I thought maybe you could stop by the fairgrounds before they're all packed up and see what kind of a read you get off of Carl Reitsma? See if you notice any inconsistencies in his story or even get a little honesty out of the guy."

"They're packing up?" This seemed odd. As far as I knew, their rides and booths were all still set up at the fairgrounds as they waited to see if they could open again. Then again, the fair had only been set to run Thursday through Sunday in the first place.

"I asked them to stick around until we solved this case, but Mr. Reitsma said if I'm not arresting him or any of his people, they should be free to go. Which is true, unfortunately. The man seems to know the law and how to make it suit him."

"So how long do we have? How long do you think it'll take them to clear out?" I reached for my sneakers and pulled them on.

"Last I heard, Reitsma told his employees to tear everything down at the campground while he headed to the fairgrounds to get things in order. He had a guy of about thirty named Ian with him."

"The floater and the longest employee," I said, remembering the name.

"Right. But neither of them know you, so I figured this could be your chance to get in there and see if you can find out anything before the others show up."

I paused, tying my shoe. "But if you've already thoroughly questioned Mr. Reitsma, what makes you think I'll find out anything different than you did?"

"Because you're not part of the police force." Jay stood as if he was getting ready to lead the way off the boat, but my armpits had broken into a sudden sweat.

This Reitsma guy sounded pretty agitated. Then again, would I rather go strike up a conversation with someone I didn't know or go interrogate one of my new witch friends from town? Neither seemed like fun options.

Jay had thought this through, though. "I figured if you went in there under the pretense of packing up the coffee truck—act like you're as angry about being shut down as they are. Maybe even say that you stood up to the police and told them if they weren't going to arrest you, it was time to pack up your coffee truck and get it out of there."

"I . . . Do you think they'll believe me?" In high school, I'd had a short stint where I got the lead in one of our school plays and I was convinced my next stop was Hollywood. Of course I'd never followed through on that. And I certainly hadn't been practicing my acting skills for the last decade.

"They have no reason not to." Jay noticed I hadn't stood yet and was hesitating. "Don't worry, Tabby. I'm not going to leave you on your own. I plan to park down the road and keep an eye on the situation. Even if Reitsma catches on that something is off, I'll be right there to intervene."

That, at least, made me feel better.

I stood. "All right. I guess we're off to the fair."

Chapter Sixteen

I STOPPED BY THE neighboring houseboat to let Rachael know I was headed out for a while and she could just drop the key through my mail slot when she was done.

"I don't know. I might still be here," she said wryly. If that was true, I could sit her down and talk to her about Sheena at that point, when we hopefully were both thinking clearly.

I opened my mouth to tell her about the stolen credit card, then stopped myself. I had enough trouble making Rachael take payment for her work as it was. She didn't need to know about the renters stiffing me.

I apologized again for the mess, then quickly skipped up to the parking lot, where Jay was waiting to follow me to the fairgrounds.

After making the short drive, I parked in the main empty lot and then kept an eye on the entrance to the fairgrounds while I gave Jay a few minutes to park down the road and get here on foot. The police tape was still up everywhere, but police security no longer seemed to be watching the place. I saw flashes of two men moving throughout the center of the fairgrounds, and in their grubby jeans and T-shirts, they looked more like carnival staff than police. That must be Carl Reitsma and his longtime employee, Ian.

When I spotted Jay near the entrance, I decided it was my time to shine. Once the carnival's work trucks had cleared out, it would be a lot easier to remove the coffee truck—if Jay actually wanted me to follow through on that. I wasn't sure I felt right about pulling down the crime scene tape to move Olivia's truck off the fairgrounds.

Jay kept his distance from me as I lifted a leg over the mess of rope and crime scene tape and then swung my other leg over. The movement caught the eyes of the two men in the center of the fairgrounds.

"Can I help you with something?" The man who called this was short with a belly that hung over his jeans, but he bellowed like he was ten feet tall. I'd seen this man around on Thursday night, and I'd known he'd been part of the carnival staff, but now as he demanded an answer from me, it was obvious he was the big boss.

"Yeah, um, I'm just here to get my truck." I waved toward the coffee truck, which could be seen in the distance.

"Your truck?" He squinted, walking toward me, but I didn't want him or the other guy to see Jay, so I marched for the coffee truck.

Jay had suggested it would work better if I acted as though I owned the coffee truck myself, and I tried as I spoke again to take on the character of a coffee truck owner. "Yeah. It's been stuck here for days, making no money at all." I fed off the anger I could feel radiating off this Reitsma guy. "Finally, I told the cops if they weren't going to arrest me, I was getting my livelihood out of here. You're with the carnival?" I asked, as though I had no idea.

"That's right. Carl Reitsma." He held out a hand to shake mine. "I'm the carnival manager."

The tall thin guy with him had yet to say a word, but he looked vaguely familiar, too. I wondered if I'd seen him at the fair Thursday or if we'd come across each other at the campground when I'd been there with Jay. I felt a trickle of sweat run down my back at the thought.

"Right. I'm Tabitha." I was about to give my last name out of habit, but something stopped me. The tall thin guy—Ian—tilted his head, like he was scrutinizing me, so I figured I'd better get the topic of conversation back on them.

"Are you here to pack up, too? Because it sure would be easier to drive my coffee truck out of here once your work trucks are out of the way." As I said this, I walked toward the half dozen large white trucks that somehow would house all of their rides and equipment.

Thankfully, they followed me over, bringing us even farther from the entry of the fairgrounds. I had no doubt that Jay would have gotten himself around the ropes and crime scene tape by now, but I had no idea if he could hear our conversation.

Regardless, I forged on. "I still can't believe there was a murder in the middle of our local fun fair. What are the odds?"

Carl tilted his head. "It's not as uncommon as you'd think."

My eyebrows shot up, and I was about to ask him if he'd ever come across a murder at one of his carnivals before, but before I could, he said, "Ian, you've got all the truck keys, right?"

Ian was still scrutinizing me with his brow furrowed. "Yeah . . ." He drew out the word.

"What do you say we move a couple of the trucks into the parking lot so this little lady can pull her coffee truck through?"

Ian looked between his boss and me, and he opened his mouth as though he was going to say something. But then his boss, apparently used to giving orders and moving on, turned his back on his employee, facing me again.

Ian gave me one more long look and then headed off toward the work truck in the back of the grouping. While I was glad to have not been outed, I still hadn't come up with any useful information, either.

I was watching Ian when Carl asked his next question. "Them local police are really somethin', aren't they?" He chuckled. "You really stood up to them?"

I had the distinct impression I was being hit on, even though this guy had to be at least forty and from out of town.

I cleared my throat. "I had no choice. I have to get my truck out of here." As I said the words, the first big carnival truck moved into the parking lot, but even as he was backing up, Ian kept his gaze trained on me. He had to recognize me from my visit to the campground.

As Carl started to follow my gaze, I spun back on him. "Hey, I was chatting with one of your employees Thursday. He gave me his email address, but I guess I misplaced it."

Carl furrowed his brow. "Oh yeah? Who's that?" He sounded perturbed by my question.

"You know, I don't even know the guy's name. But he had a blue streak in his hair?" I motioned to my own red hair. "I really liked the color and he said if I emailed him, he'd let me know where he got the dye."

Carl's eyes narrowed at me, and I wondered what I'd said wrong. "Danny's not with us anymore."

My eyes widened. Had there been two murders since Thursday night? Or had something else happened to Danny?

But Carl must have sensed something over the top in my reaction, because a second later, he chuckled and added, "I had to let Danny go. He hadn't done his job properly since I first hired the guy. Always wandering away from his post in the middle of his shift."

I had a name for the carnie who was definitely in charge of taking care of the one attraction that had traces of blood in it, but he had suddenly been fired? That definitely seemed suspicious. Then again, if what Carl Reitsma was saying was true, and Danny had wandered away from his post, anyone could have gotten into the fun house without being seen, which would leave us without any witnesses at all.

"Wow, that surprises me," I said as I processed all of this. "He seemed pretty diligent when I was talking to him."

Carl let out another humorless chuckle, relaxed enough that he either wasn't hiding anything or he was a very good actor. "If he'd a been doing his job, he wouldn't a had time to stand around talking to the coffee lady, though, now would he?"

He had a point there. Ian had moved the second carnival truck by this time, leaving a small opening toward the parking lot that would just barely allow for me to drive the coffee truck through—if I was comfortable driving a coffee truck. He headed back our way, so I knew I didn't have long to dig into this information.

"I'm sorry Danny didn't work out, but I'd still love to get his email address or a phone number if you have one."

I'd barely gotten my question out when Ian held out a finger pointed toward me as he strode straight for us. "That lady's been poking around out at the campground, Carl. I hope you're keeping aware of what you're saying to her."

My mouth went dry, especially when Carl spun on me, his eyebrows so contorted, they were practically joined.

"Is that a fact?" Carl's hand darted out and grabbed my wrist. "Don't worry, hon. I always know I can count on my carnies to protect me."

But I was worried. I was very worried because as he took a step closer to me, getting right in my face, I didn't see Jay anywhere at all.

Chapter Seventeen

"Wait, that's where I know you from?" I put on my ditsiest voice as I pointed at Ian and tried to pretend that Carl's death grip on my arm wasn't bothering me one bit. "Yeah, I live right near Camperland and my cat wanders over there all the time." I only hoped that word hadn't spread too far and wide that I actually lived at the marina.

Ian narrowed his eyes at me but spoke to his boss. "She did have a cat with her," he said begrudgingly.

I nodded like I'd had too much caffeine. Carl's eyebrows were still contorted, but I felt him starting to soften toward me, at least to the point that he wasn't going to drag me away somewhere never to be seen again.

In an instant, I realized this could be my only shot at getting away. If Jay wasn't going to get me out of this, I clearly had to take care of myself. "Listen, I really should get my coffee truck packed up." I took a step away, and thankfully, Carl let his hand fall away from my arm. "I really appreciate you moving the trucks, and I should be out of your hair in no time at all."

I hadn't stuck around long enough to find out any useful information, aside from blue-haired Danny's first name and employment status, but I wasn't willing to put my life in jeopardy to figure out further details. As soon as Carl's hand left my arm, I spun and marched purposefully away from the two carnival workers and toward Olivia's coffee truck.

Only as I trekked in that direction did I realize that to follow through on actually removing the coffee truck, that would entail me having the keys. Which I did not.

We always kept the back unlocked, so I made a show of going aboard. The serving window had been left open, I supposed because Olivia had been instructed to leave immediately Thursday, so it didn't even give me a chance to get out of view of Carl and Ian and catch my breath. They continued to watch me, and as I moved coffee supplies back to their cupboards, I knew they were still discussing whether or not my story was believable.

But then, quite suddenly, their gazes darted toward the fair entrance. That was when I finally saw Jay stepping over the police tape and striding onto the fairgrounds with his cell phone held to his ear.

Was that why he hadn't been around to protect me? He had gone off to take a phone call?

But before I could process any of this, he hung up and called out, "I'll ask you all to stop packing up right now, please."

Jay said this to Carl and Ian, then glanced at me as though his words were directed at all of us. "I realize you're all in a hurry to get out of here, but we have some new evidence in the case, and I'm afraid with the implication, I'll have to ask everything to remain exactly where it is for further investigation."

Carl marched straight for him, flailing his arms as he went. "What kind of evidence could possibly make any difference at this point?"

I left the safe cubby of the coffee truck to head toward the group.

"We've found a DNA match to the victim, and it involves one of your attractions," Jay told Carl.

Carl's hands flew up again. "I'm sure you found plenty of DNA on the Ferris wheel. So what! It doesn't mean me or my people were responsible for the guy's death."

"No, but the fact that we found his DNA in the fun house leaves us curious to know why none of your employees claimed to have been near there. At the very least, it leads me to believe your workers are covering for the person at fault. Now I'll need the names of all your employees who worked in and around the fun house on Thursday night."

I felt Ian scrutinizing me again, as though seeing me with Jay was bringing back the memory that I had been with him at the campground, too. Plus, it would have to seem coincidental to Carl that I'd just been asking questions about Danny. Rather than volunteering this information in front of them, I took this as my cue to leave. "I guess if I can't get the coffee truck out, I'll wait for you to tell me when I can," I told Jay, looking at the ground so I wouldn't give myself away to any of them. I strode quickly toward the parking lot, fully aware that I was giving up far too easily compared to how seemingly indignant I'd been when I arrived.

But I didn't care. This was too stressful, and Jay had not been around as he had promised.

I was all the way to the parking lot before I let out my breath.

Chapter Eighteen

I WONDERED WHAT HAD transpired with Carl and Ian at the fairgrounds as I waited to hear from Jay at the houseboat. Had he had to arrest them? Whatever the case, I was much happier to hear about it after the fact.

I shot off a text, letting him know where I was. Unfortunately, Rachael had finished cleaning the neighboring houseboat and had left while I was gone. I paced the front deck with my eyes on the marina parking lot, toying with the sea glass around my neck and trying to calm down from the trouble I'd almost gotten myself in.

Thankfully, I didn't have to wait long. Ten minutes later, Jay pulled into the marina lot and parked beside Frank's truck.

Sherlock, who had also been pacing the front deck, sniffed the air, catching Jay's scent, and let out a mreow as he stepped aboard the gangplank.

"Oh, good," he said. "I hoped you were okay when you left the fairgrounds."

"I almost wasn't. Ian recognized me from the campground." His eyes widened, but I couldn't leave him on the hook for this for too long. "I made up an excuse and said I lived near there. But once you brought up the DNA match and had them scrambling, I didn't want to stick around any longer than I had to."

Jay nodded. "The good part is that with the DNA information, I had no problem getting a judge to freeze the carnival's assets. Carl Reitsma wasn't happy about it one bit, but he won't have any recourse for the moment. I just had to wait around for an officer to show up and secure the place. Plus, I've subpoenaed all of his employee records, which he has to get to me by end of day."

"You should look into an employee named Danny," I told him. "Apparently, he ran the fun house and was fired after Thursday. He was the one I told you about with the blue streak in his hair."

"Fired? Really?" Jay made a note as I opened the houseboat door to let us inside. He followed me in, as did Sherlock. While Jay and I took the two seats at the table, my cat strode straight for the mess of detective novels on the floor and perched his front paws on one. When we were alone, I'd ask him if he was looking for something specific.

"I couldn't get any more details before Ian came back and recognized me. What about Sheena Park?" I asked. "While you wait for the employee records, could you talk to her?"

"Good idea." Jay scribbled quick notes as I spoke. "You've got a real knack for this, Tabby. Have you ever thought of going into private detective work?"

I laughed like he was joking, but he didn't laugh along. "I've got my hands full at the moment between the café and houseboat renters who are trying to scam their way out of paying."

Jay nibbled his lip. "Sorry. I haven't had time to follow up on that."

I shook my head. I hadn't meant to put pressure on him by bringing it up. "Believe me, I know a murder case is higher on the priority list."

He stood. "Interested in paying a surprise visit to Sheena Park with me?"

I'd barely sat down, but you'd better believe I wanted to find out if she was truly involved in Bryan Klaus's murder. "You bet. Can we bring Sherlock?"

I'd been to Sheena Park's apartment once before. That time, I'd had both Jay and Aaron with me as we questioned Sheena's sister's boyfriend. The two had since broken up, or so I'd heard, but today we were here for Sheena herself.

Jay led the way across the street to the apartment building, which had outside stairwells so we could arrive right at her door without warning.

Sheena swung open the door to Jay's knock with a look of surprise, which promptly morphed into a strained smile. "Oh. Detective Jameson? Tabby?" She glanced down at Sherlock for a second, but I sensed that seeing me with a cat relaxed her, if only a little. "What can I help you with?"

"I had some further questions for you about Thursday night at the summer fair," Jay told her. "May we come in?"

Sheena glanced again at Sherlock. With her sharp head motions, her short curly hair bounced. "Oh, I'd love to, but Judy's allergic."

I opened my mouth to say that Sherlock and I could wait outside. It was the first time this had been any kind of an issue. The cat was purring in my arms, which in the past had indicated he trusted people in the vicinity.

I hoped that was the case with Sheena, but before I could actually say anything, Jay said, "No problem. We can talk right here." Her smile tensed again. I wondered if she thought the cat allergy might have gotten her out of being questioned altogether. "Through our interviews, we've heard indications that you had planned to vandalize the summer fair on Thursday night. Is that true?"

Sheena's eyes widened and she looked again to me, as though she either thought I had been the one to throw her under the bus or that I might save her from this question. I admit, I was surprised at how blunt Jay's first question was, but I could also sense his eagerness. He knew we were close to some answers and didn't want to waste time.

It was a long moment before Sheena offered a careful response. "Who did you hear this from?"

"I can't tell you that, Miss Park. But I can tell you that we have strong reasons to believe this is true." Jay's gentle tone and good looks seemed to make Sheena believe his words, even though it was a nonanswer.

"I—I guess I had joked about it."

"But you didn't actually do it?" Jay didn't stop there. "You didn't actually pour soda in the fun house mirror maze or tamper with any electrical wiring?"

Another interminable pause, where Sheena seemed to weigh her options. If Jay knew such specifics, how much else would he know?

Finally, she said, "Why don't you both come in."

I looked down at Sherlock, still purring in my arms.

She shook her head. "Judy'll be fine."

This made me wonder if Judy's allergy had been a lie or if it was mild in comparison to the upheaval Sheena might experience if her neighbors heard this discussion.

I felt slightly guilty, but I followed Jay inside, torn between trying to keep my cat from shedding dander and wanting to let him explore. However, by the time we made it to Sheena's small living room,

Sherlock made up his mind for me, as he appeared to be fast asleep in my arms.

If this was any indication of anything, I had to take it to mean that there was nothing important to learn here. Didn't I? I reached for my sea glass, but it didn't seem especially warm or cold.

And then I promptly started to doubt its magical abilities altogether. Sheena had as much as admitted she'd vandalized the fun house on Thursday night. She'd been angry with Bryan Klaus. How could we not be on the right track? I willed the sea glass to warm between my fingers, but still nothing happened.

Jay knocked me out of my thoughts when he returned to his agenda. "Would you like to tell me the specifics of what you vandalized at the fair on Thursday night, or am I going to have to interrogate you all afternoon until I get to the truth?"

The question sounded rhetorical, and Sheena took it that way. She nodded, looking at her lap. "It's true that I bought a soda and some ice cream with caramel sauce and emptied them inside the maze of mirrors in the fun house." She looked up at Jay. "But I swear, as much as I hated Bryan Klaus and wanted to interrupt his fair's success, I didn't go near the guy." Her words sounded desperate, and I was tempted to believe her.

"Is there any reason you can think of that we would have found Mr. Klaus's blood mixed in with your spilled soda in the maze of mirrors?" Jay asked. He certainly wasn't holding back. Even with his gentle tone, this sounded like blame.

Sheena pulled back, her eyebrows immediately contorting. "What? No, of course not." She fidgeted with her hands as she quickly processed this information and how guilty it made her seem. "Ruth was there with me! She'll tell you that I spilled a large soda and the creamy caramel and then we were out of there."

"And did Ruth help with that?"

Sheena shook her head. I felt as though all of her responses now were instinctive and purely honest. Plus, Sherlock was still sleeping and my sea glass hung limp and unaffected around my neck. "No, she wouldn't actually do it, but unlike Rachael, who insisted on waiting outside, she was glad I was doing it. She'll tell you, we just walked through the fun house once, super quickly, and we didn't see Klaus at all. Well, not until later."

"Where did you see him?" Jay asked the question I was thinking.

"He was yelling at one of his employees. Something about leaving a booth unattended."

"Do you know which booth?" I asked before I could hold myself back. Jay nodded, letting my question stand.

But Sheena just shrugged. "I couldn't say. We rushed past him as soon as we saw he was occupied."

"You rushed past to vandalize something else within the fair?"

Sheena looked at her lap again, avoiding Jay's eyes and his question.

"Look, Miss Park, if you didn't have anything to do with Mr. Klaus's murder on Thursday night, I suggest you tell me everything you know, as plainly and completely as possible. Anything you hold back right now will only cause more guilt to be shed on you and possibly your friends who were with you that night."

That was all it took to get her talking. Unfortunately, there wasn't much else to tell. "I had hoped to cut the electricity to some of the rides, but they all had lockboxes with safety mechanisms and I was afraid if I didn't know what I was doing, I might electrocute myself. But when we went on the Ferris wheel, I saw my chance and I broke a control lever while the ride operator was busy away from his platform. I was sure he'd have to at least shut down that ride, but the guy seemed to know a way to work around the broken control. We had skipped out of line by then, but he had the ride up and running within a few minutes. I got so frustrated, but Rachael calmed me down and Ruth gave me some lavender oil, and then we just decided to forget about Klaus and have fun. I swear, I didn't even touch any of the Ferris wheel cars that he was found on that night. You can check for my fingerprints." She held out her palms, as though Jay might be able to check for a match right here and now.

"And I'll be able to confirm this information with Ruth Boudreau and Rachael Adams?" Jay asked.

Sheena nodded. "They'll tell you the same thing. I swear."

While I didn't love the fact that Rachael had kept this from me when I'd thought we were becoming friends, I did respect the witches' protectiveness over one another. And I was glad Sheena seemed to have eyewitnesses who could confirm her innocence—at least innocence of murder.

Just then, Jay's cell phone rang. He pulled it out, took one look at it, and then said, "I have to take this. Meet you at the car?"

I didn't love facing up to Sheena alone as Jay left us, but she was surprisingly gracious when I told her, "Don't worry. If you had nothing to do with Mr. Klaus's murder, Jay will figure out ways to confirm it. But if you think of anything else that you might have seen or that could be important, would you call us?"

Sheena nodded and led the way to her apartment door. "Am I going to get in trouble for the vandalism?"

I didn't know for sure how to answer that, but I said, "I think finding a murderer is all that's at the forefront for the police right now. Just be honest, help them wherever you can, and you'll be fine."

Jay's call had been from Aaron, calling him back to the station.

"I hope that means the carnival's employee records have shown up," he said as he drove me back to the marina.

As I got out of his unmarked police car, Frank was just heading up from his office toward his truck.

"Oh, hey, Tabby. Hi, Detective Jameson," he said, turning to face me. "I rigged some of your lights better. Was afraid they were going to fall into the water."

I glanced over his shoulder, but I could only see one from here. "Oh, great. Thanks."

"Hopefully those Marshalls haven't been giving you too much hassle about it."

"Millers," I told him.

He furrowed his brow. "What's that?"

"It was John and Julie Miller." But as I said their names, I remembered those probably weren't their real names.

Frank confirmed this when he said, "No, I mean the couple staying in the Peterson's houseboat. Jason and Julie Marshall."

Now I furrowed my brow. John and Julie Miller had been staying in the Peterson's houseboat. "Wait, you talked to the renters? They told you their names were Jason and Julie Marshall?" The name Marshall was familiar, but I couldn't place it.

Jay's got out of his car and his brow furrowed. "You're sure it was them?"

"Yeah," Frank told Jay. Then he turned back to me. "They didn't have to introduce themselves. I knew 'em from when they used to live in Crystal Cove."

Jay turned to me. "Are you telling me that the Millers who scammed you with a fake credit card were actually Jason and Julie Marshall?"

I shrugged. Even though the question appeared to be for me, I had no idea who these Marshall people were.

"The Marshalls scammed you with a fake credit card?" Frank scoffed and shook his head. "Shouldn't be surprised. They were always cheapskates, even when they owned the bar over on Eighth."

Jay looked as though his brain was turning at a million miles a minute. So was mine. I'd just been over on Eighth Street yesterday.

Before I could put it together, though, I asked, "What?" too eager to wait for my brain to catch up.

"That bar they used to own? It was foreclosed on about five years ago."

"Okay. Good reason for being broke, but . . ." I said in way of a lead-in because I knew there was more. It was right on the tip of my tongue.

"It's now Crystal Cove's local mini golf course. Taken over by Bryan Klaus."

Chapter Nineteen

RATHER THAN HEADING TO my houseboat, I got back into Jay's car, and we went straight to the police station.

On the way, I poked holes, as though I was trying to prove the scamming renters' innocence. "But they hadn't even known there was a summer fair. Plus, Frank said he'd seen them going out Thursday night just after ten." I pulled my spreadsheet up on my phone to confirm the time. "They had an alibi. They couldn't have been at the fair to kill Klaus."

"Maybe not." Jay pulled into the police department's lot. "But with such a strong motive and the timing of their visit, we'll definitely take a good look at them. Providing we can find them," he added.

I was getting to know Samantha Reese, the Crystal Cove Police Department's receptionist. She was the one person in the police department who didn't look at me funny for bringing my cat everywhere I went. She was in her fifties with graying hair and a warm smile. She always bent in close to say hello to Sherlock and scratch behind his ears. If I had to put money on it, I would guess she had three or four cats of her own at home.

But today as she bent in toward Sherlock, Jay said, "Tabby? Are you coming?"

I usually didn't get invited beyond the front reception office, but I was glad to be asked. I gave Samantha a quick second to say hello to Sherlock while offering Jay a nod and saying, "You bet."

Jay's desk was in the middle of a busy open office. I'd met several people on the small police force since moving to town, but none of them acknowledged me today, clearly focused on their own work.

Jay swept a chair away from a nearby empty desk over to his and held out a hand toward it. I sat and glanced around, wondering which desk was Aaron's, or if he had his own office.

No sooner was I seated than Jay had the receiver from his desk phone in his hand. When someone picked up on the other end, he spoke quickly. "Yes, it's Jameson from Crystal Cove, Oregon. I'm looking for a car rental, possibly from Seattle, under the names Jason or Julie Marshall, or possibly John and Julie Miller." He rattled off the letters "JOY" from the license plate number I'd gotten. As he spoke, he typed into a laptop. "Sure, I'll hold." As soon as he was on hold, he looked over to me. "Seattle P.D. will be able to look into this a lot quicker than I can. In the meantime, I'm putting out an APB for their rental car throughout Oregon, Washington, and California. What time did you say they left today?"

"Probably by noon?" I asked it as a question, now doubting the time. But Jay made a note and relayed this information as someone came back onto the phone line with him.

"Right, okay. I'll wait to hear back." He rattled off his cell phone number and then hung up. It immediately rang again in his hand.

"What's up, Thom?" he said in way of an answer. He nodded several times and made more notes before hanging up without so much as a goodbye. I was getting used to their curt ways with each other.

"Did he find out something?" Even though it wasn't my place to ask, I couldn't help myself. The stern, focused look on Jay's face told me he did.

"Reitsma dropped off the employee records, and Thom was able to catch up with Danny at his sister's house, not far from Crystal Cove."

"What did Danny say? Was he really fired for leaving his station outside the fun house?"

"He doesn't think so. And he wasn't fired Thursday night. He said if it had been a matter of him not being at his post, his boss would have canned him right then and there. It was actually yesterday afternoon when Reitsma told him he was out of a job. He doesn't believe it's from incompetence at all, but something to do with the police investigation, but he says he doesn't know anything else. All he could tell Detective Thom was that when he returned from grabbing a hot dog Thursday night, some idiot had made a mess of the hall of mirrors and he had to shut the fun house down."

Jay's phone rang again, and he held up a finger to me as he answered and took down more details. After hanging up, he said, "Come on. We have to go. They found Jason and Julie Marshall's rental vehicle, and they're not far from here."

I had to admit, I was surprised to hear they hadn't gone far. I expected they'd already have returned to Washington by the time the police caught up with them.

They would have almost had time by this point, too.

"But if he wasn't fired until yesterday, where was he when we went to the campground? Or when the police first interviewed all the employees?" I jogged around the car and slid into the passenger seat.

Jay started driving, shaking his head. "Apparently one of the new carnies was warning people to get out of sight when the police showed up."

"New carnies?" Had Grady truly been trying to distract us while giving his coworkers a warning—as if to earn his place among the group? Or had it been Kevin?

"Danny said he didn't know the name of the new carnie. He could be covering for him." Jay didn't bother trying to figure this out for the moment. "Apparently, the Marshalls booked in at a motel not far away and their rental car is in the motel lot." Jay turned off the highway into the Crystal Motel parking lot. We'd just passed Camperland and were still within the town limits of Crystal Cove.

"Wait, when you said they're not far, you can't mean here?"

Jay nodded with raised eyebrows. Strangely, my first thought was a concern for having dissatisfied customers who had felt the need to leave a beautiful houseboat to check in to this dive of a motel. But then I rolled my eyes at myself and remembered how Jason or John or whoever he was had given me a stolen credit card. The surprising part was that he'd stuck around town to get caught.

Jay parked, and I followed him into the motel's small front office near the highway. A slight Asian lady in her sixties greeted us across the dingy turquoise counter. "Can I help you?"

"Yes, I understand you have a couple who just checked in today, driving a white Chrysler?"

The lady moved a few feet over to a desktop computer and scrolled through what seemed like a few screens full of data, then turned back to Jay. "We don't keep car brands listed."

Wouldn't she have known that before taking the time to look it up? Was she stalling?

Jay must have wondered the same thing because he got right to the point. He laid his police badge out on her counter and said, "Listen, ma'am, I'll need you to give me a list of every person who has checked in today and which room they are residing in."

The lady knew he meant business. She headed for her computer and a minute later came back with one name scrawled on a piece of paper. "Only one check-in. John Miller."

So he was still trying to use the same stolen credit card, right here in town. Seemed awfully daring. Why stick around so close to town? Did they not think I would report the stolen card? Did they think I was made of money and could withstand a renter not paying when I'd barely started renting out houseboats?

I was so caught up in my own drama that at first I didn't know what was happening when the lady from the office rounded her counter and headed for the front glass door. But then I saw the key in her hand.

We were about to confront Jason and Julie Marshall and find out exactly why they'd come to Crystal Cove.

I wasn't sure what Jay, the expert, thought, but the fact that they'd stuck around and not raced out of town made me think they'd have to be pretty fearless, or pretty stupid, if they were actual murderers.

Chapter Twenty

Unfortunately, there was no answer when we knocked on room 214, where the Marshalls were apparently staying.

The Asian lady knocked three times, calling out, "Mr. Miller? Please open the door!" but I didn't hear a single sound from inside.

"Can you open it?" Jay motioned to the key in her hand.

There was no DO NOT DISTURB sign on room 214, so the lady hesitated, flipping the small gold key over in her hands several times. Most motels that I'd stayed at had upgraded to a key card system, but this rundown place seemed as though it hadn't had any upgrades done in the past two decades.

Finally, the clerk knocked one more time, but this time called, "Housekeeping!" as she inserted her key into the lock. A second later, she opened the door to an empty room. Two closed suitcases sat on the foot of a queen bed. Otherwise, the room appeared untouched.

"Where have they gone?" Jay asked aloud, as if to himself. He took a step toward the open doorway, but the clerk stepped into his path.

"No, mister. Not without a warrant." She sounded as though this wasn't the first time she'd said these words.

I looked out over the balcony rail, toward the rocky seashore that wasn't quite within view. Then to the highway and, finally, to the parking lot.

The dive motel seemed like the kind of out-of-the-way place that a criminal could hide out—close enough to the highway for a quick getaway, yet far enough from any enjoyable local amenities that it wouldn't be overrun by tourists.

My eyes settled on the white sedan—one of only five cars in the motel's small lot. My sea glass warmed, and another thought came to me. I spoke the words before I'd fully gotten them through my head. "I think I know where they've gone."

I didn't know, of course, and as soon as we left the clerk at her office and I stopped to retrieve Sherlock from Jay's vehicle, Jay asked me, "Tabby? Where are we going?"

I shook my head. "Camperland is so close. Do you think that's a coincidence?" I, for one, did not.

"Hmm. You're right. Do you think the Marshalls have some connection with the carnies from out of town?"

I shrugged. "They've all been shady and dishonest with you. And why?" I thought through everyone I had met in the past week. "I'd figured the houseboat renters were just here looking for a free getaway, but the fact that Bryan Klaus put them out of business a few years ago? You're right. That certainly gives them a strong motive."

Jay continued my path of theorizing as we walked out of the motel parking lot and north along the highway. "If they still kept in touch with people from town, perhaps other business owners from the Crystal Cove Business Association, they would have heard that Bryan Klaus was running the summer fair on his own this year."

"And acting pigheaded about it." I snapped my mouth shut, not wanting to speak ill of the dead, but Jay didn't seem to notice.

"What if the Marshalls planted an employee among the carnival staff? Didn't Grady say he was the newest employee? And he had come back to me with a different story about which booth he worked at." Jay sounded more convinced, the more he spoke. "I'll bet it had nothing to do with Carl Reitsma. I'll bet he went back to the Marshalls to collect whatever payout they'd promised him, and they'd told him that to prove his innocence, he'd better claim he was working at the hot dog stand that night."

"Just like everyone else claimed," I reminded Jay as the Camperland sign came into view another fifty feet down the highway. "I didn't get the feeling Grady was guilty of much besides running away. And if all the carnies were claiming to have been working the hot dog stand on Thursday night, weren't they all lying, except Grady? At least at first." Hiking along a highway with a squirmy cat in my arms was no easy feat. Maybe we should have brought Jay's car.

Just as I thought this, Sherlock wriggled free and launched himself from my arms. I wasn't comfortable having him out on his own so close to the highway, but at the same time, there wasn't a lot of traffic at the moment and it looked as though he was headed through the long grass on the side of the road, straight for the campground.

"Sherlock seems to think the campground is where we'll find our answers," Jay said.

But then I thought of something else. "I don't know for sure that it was him, but I thought I'd seen the carnie with the red baseball cap near the marina the other day. I thought he might have been there to threaten me for asking questions at the campground, but the thought also crossed my mind that he was there to see the Millers . . . I mean, the Marshalls."

"Kevin." Jay stopped in place, pulled out his phone, and scrolled through his notes, looking for Kevin's last name. When he found it, he looked up at me with wide eyes. "His name is Kevin Marshall."

Chapter Twenty-one

JAY AND I WERE discussing how to make a stealthy approach to the campground when I caught movement out of the corner of my eye. In a knee-jerk reaction, I pulled him off the side of the road toward the large trunk of a nearby oak tree.

"I think the Marshalls are leaving the campground," I whispered, hoping my quick glance had it correct.

"They'll be headed this direction," Jay whispered back. He pulled out his phone, and his thumbs flew over the keyboard furiously.

It wasn't long before we heard voices. The tree we were hiding behind was butted up against a wooden fence that sectioned off a small parcel of land belonging to a farmhouse.

We wouldn't be able to stay out of sight for much longer without somehow trying to scale the fence, but before I could suggest this, Jay held up a hand to hold me back and then stepped the other direction, out into plain view.

"Mr. and Mrs. Marshall?"

The voice I knew as Mr. Miller's spoke up. "What is this? Were you spying on us?" He sounded like he was speaking through gritted teeth, and although I couldn't see him from my vantage point, I could picture him with his politician's smile—which, now that I thought about it, was probably just a smile to cover over his transgressions.

"No, no, sir." Jay's voice was easy and relaxed. I admired him for his ability to act casual, even when it seemed we were closing in on a murderer. "I tracked your vehicle down at the Crystal Motel, and I wanted to ask you a few questions before you left town."

"What is this about?" Jason Marshall asked. I could picture him trying to intimidate Jay the same way he'd tried to intimidate me about getting a kickback from the houseboat rental price.

But Jay wasn't having it. "I have some questions about your whereabouts this past Thursday evening."

"Thursday evening?" There was panic behind Julie's words. "We got into town late that night."

"Let's head to your motel room. We can talk there."

As they started to move in that direction, I was suddenly aware that there was nowhere for me to hide where I wouldn't be visible within a dozen of their steps. I was about to reveal myself and had barely taken a step around the tree's trunk when Jay turned the Marshalls toward their motel and waved a hand behind his back, which I had to assume was a signal meant for me.

Was he telling me to stay hidden? Or waving me toward the campground? That was what it looked like, but why?

What did he expect me to accomplish all on my own, with my only backup a nosy, investigative cat?

Speaking of which . . . I couldn't see Sherlock anywhere.

While the Marshalls' backs were to me, I quickly skirted around the tree trunk to the other side, so I'd stay out of their view as they continued walking toward the motel.

"I have another officer headed for the campground," Jay told them, and I wondered if this could somehow be true, if that was who he'd been texting, or if he meant me.

No. That would truly be ridiculous. I was sure he only wanted me to watch the campground from the sidelines to see if Kevin Marshall was up to anything suspicious.

"Why would they go to the campground?" Julie said in such a loud voice, it was almost a shriek. "Anything you need, I'm sure we can help you with." They were the words of a worried mother.

If she had an instant to let her son know, surely he would run before any police could get to him. I only hoped Jay could stop her from having any opportunity to notify her son, because no matter how skilled Jay seemed to think I was with investigations, I wouldn't be able to stop a twentysomething guy from getting away, especially if he was surrounded by his protective coworkers.

Or maybe . . . I pulled out my cell phone as another thought occurred to me.

Maybe Jay had meant that there would be police on their way if I requested backup.

I scrolled to Aaron's contact, and he picked up on the first ring. "Aaron, it's Tabby," I whispered.

"What's wrong?" I was glad he could read the panic in my tone. He was an astute detective, and that was what I needed right now.

"I'm on the highway near Camperland. Jay is questioning Jason and Julie Marshall at the Crystal Motel, but we have reason to suspect their son was working with the carnival and the three may have conspired to kill Bryan Klaus. We need backup at the campground as soon as possible."

"We?"

I held back a frustrated groan. Leave it to Aaron to latch onto the one word that made his jealousy rear its head. In college, I'd had a jealous boyfriend who had been cheated on in the past, and it made him unable to think clearly. He was constantly accusing me of not being the person I claimed to be or not being where I said I was going. It was exhausting, and in this moment, I decided that if I ever chose to date a man in Crystal Cove, it would not be Aaron Thom.

"I got a garbled text from Jay that I couldn't make any sense of," Aaron went on. He sounded casual, like he planned on taking his time if Jay had taken charge of this part of the investigation.

I held back my sigh and got to the point. "The Marshalls stayed at one of my rental houseboats under a fake name. Detective Jameson was helping me follow up on that when it led back to connections to the murder investigation. I hope you're on your way," I added.

"I am," he told me, switching to his usual curt business tone. "I'll be there soon."

I only hoped that was true and his jealousy, or his need to prove his superiority to Jay, didn't get the better of him.

Chapter Twenty-two

I CREPT TOWARD THE Camperland entrance slowly, hoping Aaron might arrive by the time I got there.

No such luck.

I stayed out of sight along the side of a large wooden Camperland sign, surveying the part of the campground within view. I could see half a dozen tents off to my left and two of the picnic tables in the central communal area, but many of the tents had been dismantled. Every few seconds, a young person moved through my vision carrying an armful of camping supplies, but none were any of the carnies I recognized, and none stayed in my view long enough to study them. It seemed they were packing up, even if they weren't allowed to take their carnival with them.

As I was lost in thought, wondering if Carl Reitsma would try to sneak his carnies in after dark to pack up the rides and booths regardless of what he'd been instructed, someone I recognized moved into my view. Sherlock. He sat on his haunches thirty feet away, right in my line of vision, as though he knew I'd see him there.

I didn't like him being around one or more carnies who had conspired to commit murder, but at the same time, I wasn't about to rush in and try to rescue him on my own.

I glanced back toward the highway. Still no sign of Aaron or any other police officers. The odd car passed on the highway, but most drivers had their eyes straight ahead on the road or off to the other side, toward the ocean. I had another pang of worry that Aaron's jealousy could rattle him so severely that he'd decide to take his time in arriving.

I shook my head. That was something my old boyfriend, Drew, might have done, but not Aaron. Aaron was too good at his job, and when it came down to it, I was pretty sure his dedication to police work trumped everything else in his life.

While I was again lost in thought, I hardly noticed Ian walk into my line of vision until he suddenly swept my cat up in one hand. He held Sherlock up over his head as though he didn't like cats or want this one too close to him.

"Hey, Grady?" he called. "Isn't this the same cat that lady had?"

The sea glass around my neck warmed as I looked around for Grady. Carl Reitsma moved into view, but I couldn't hear his response to Ian as he motioned to the ground.

Ian looked around and added, "I don't like it. I'll bet she's hanging around again."

He no sooner had the words out of his mouth when two hands grabbed me from behind my back, one around my shoulders and the other over my mouth. I tried to shriek, but the sound was muffled by his hand.

"Yep, she's hanging around all right. Just like she was hanging around with that cop."

I couldn't see much as the carnie dragged me toward the center circle of picnic tables, but the flash of a red had couldn't be mistaken.

It was Kevin Marshall. I only hoped he hadn't gotten a warning from his parents, who must be at the motel down the road by now.

My sea glass grew hotter by the second and I realized why. While I thought the warming had been nudging me to look for clues, I'd had it wrong. It had been sending me a warning.

A warning for my safety that I'd completely missed.

Chapter Twenty-three

"Ow! STUPID CAT!" IAN released Sherlock and then rubbed his scratched arm as Kevin pushed me toward the picnic tables. Blood started to bean on Ian's forearm. "What are you doin', man?" he asked Kevin. "Just give her the stupid cat and get her out of here."

"Uh-uh." Kevin pushed me passed the picnic tables toward Carl Reitsma. "I gotta talk to you, boss."

"Let me guess." Carl Reitsma let out a condescending chuckle at Kevin. "You want another one of your secret meetings to try and get nosy people away from our business? How'd that work out with the cops? Now they won't leave us alone!" He took one look at me, then my cat, and scowled back at Kevin. "I agree with Ian. Get her outta here. She's just a neighborhood lookie-loo, and we don't need none of those around here during a murder investigation. Them cops seem to think they have enough reason to implicate us already, thanks to all the lyin' you had everyone doin'."

Kevin stared at Carl for several long seconds and then turned and shoved me toward the campground exit. He didn't let go of my arms, though, apparently determined to escort me completely off the property.

I was tempted to call after Sherlock but decided quickly that the cat would have to fend for himself. I wasn't about to say a word that might keep me here a second longer than I needed to be.

But when we got to the campground exit, Kevin still didn't let go of my arms. In fact, it was a good thing there was no traffic on the highway at the moment because he shoved me all the way to the center of it and then across it.

"What? Where are you taking me?" As a quick reaction, I angled away from the motel and toward town, doing my best to motion with my elbow. "My car. It's down that way."

But Kevin didn't stop. And, in fact, before the next car passed on the highway behind us, he had nudged me onto a rocky beach across the road from the campground and pretty much out of view.

This wasn't the type of beach that brought in tourists. With rocks the size of suitcases, there wasn't any cleared area to sit and relax, and walking on them was even more of a problem.

That didn't seem to stop Kevin, though.

"Where are you taking me?" I asked again. I looked both ways, but there was nowhere to go from here. The beach—if you could call it that—was only fifty feet wide, with a steep rock face climbing up in either direction.

There was only straight ahead. There was only the ocean.

Kevin confirmed this. "It's a nice evening for a swim, right?" He gave me a hard push. It was getting dark, and even if it had been a warm enough day for a swim in the cold ocean, it wasn't the time or place to go swimming now.

In pure desperation, I blurted, "Detective Jameson has your parents!"

This stopped him, at least momentarily. "What are you talking about?" His voice sounded testing, like he didn't truly believe I even knew who his parents were.

But I did, and now that I'd brought Jay into the situation, I figured why not use it to my advantage. "That's right. Jason and Julie Marshall?" I didn't wait for a confirmation. "He has them at their motel room right now, right this second." I motioned with my chin in that direction.

He spun me around to face him. "What's he got on them?"

The truth was, I didn't know if we had anything beyond circumstantial evidence. But my sea glass was still burning hot, and I sensed now wasn't the time to admit that. "Whatever it is, it must be pretty strong evidence for him to have tracked them down out here. He definitely has them on credit card fraud from the houseboat they rented." The moment I said the words, I regretted them. They instantly took the gravity from the air, I could feel it.

"That's where I know you from." His scowl deepened, making him look older, even though I suspected he was in his early twenties or even late teens. He turned me and pushed me again toward the ocean, but this time I wasn't ready for the uneven terrain and tripped on the next rock, falling hard onto my knees.

"Get up, you little swindler!" He kicked me, hard enough it made me wince. "You playing some sort of neighbor to spy around the campground? Carl and Ian mighta believed it, but at least I went with my gut. Now it's clear you're working with that cop, but it doesn't matter because you're not going to be talking to anyone else here in a minute." He loomed over me, making his words sound extra ominous. "So why don't you tell me right now what you and the cop know about Klaus's death."

Chapter Twenty-four

"You killed him. You must have!" My words came out desperate. Was he really going to force me into the ocean, where I didn't have anything within view to swim to?

But I was a good swimmer. When I was sixteen, I'd taken the lifeguard program at our local pool in Portland. Even if he forced me into the water beyond where I could touch, even if he stayed and watched me, I could dive underwater and get out of his reach. I was pretty sure of it.

I looked up toward the highway, but we'd taken an angle toward the water and I couldn't see it from here.

"Help!" I called out anyway.

I'd barely gotten the word out when Kevin knocked me onto my back and shut me up with a hard foot on my stomach. My head hit a rock, and I feel a coolness that could have been from the rock or from seeping blood.

"Shut up!" he hissed. "If you're not going to talk, it's time to go swimming." With that, he pulled out a switchblade and held it out above me.

My eyes widened. Who knew if it was the same sharp object that had killed Bryan Klaus, but I suddenly had no doubt he planned to use it on me. The sea glass cooled around my neck as his plan became clear.

Right. He was going to make certain I couldn't swim anywhere before tossing me into the current.

As he leaned toward me with the knife, I yelled, "Wait! I'll talk. I'll talk. What do you want to know?"

He let out a humorless laugh. "For one, what does this detective have on my parents?"

I thought fast. I wanted to make it sound as though Jay had some serious evidence, but at the same time, the more hurried Kevin felt to get back to his parents, the faster he was going to use that knife on me. "A lot less than he has on you. He knows Bryan Klaus put them out of business five years ago and humiliated them."

"He humiliated all of us." Kevin dug his foot into my stomach, and by the pained look on his face, I wondered what kind of memories he was reliving, probably from his high school or even middle school years.

In my panic to somehow make this true, I said, "I'm pretty sure he's just following up on some questions before he comes after you." Before Kevin could respond, I added, "But I could talk to him! If you didn't do it, I can make sure he knows that—"

Another humorless laugh.

"Or if you did do it, I'll help you get away. He's still at the motel and my car's not far, just down the road that way. You can borrow—or you can have it!" Again, I motioned with my chin toward town, hoping somehow he'd believe my lies, hoping I'd at least get away from the water and the rocks and get him to put his knife away, if only temporarily.

But he ran a thumb along the blade of his knife and gave an extra push to my stomach with his foot. "Nah, that's not going to work. You've been hanging around too much, and I'll bet if I needed to, I could just go find your car and take it all on my own."

He raised the hand with the knife, and my eyes widened. I squirmed to the right and then to the left, the rock digging into my back, but the more I squirmed, the harder he pushed with his foot.

If I could get to the water, I still had a chance to swim out of reach. I looked toward it hopefully. I used all my strength to try to pull his foot off me, but his leg was much stronger than both my arms.

When it seemed I had no recourse at all, I grasped for my cool sea glass with both hands and shut my eyes. I'd been playing around with magic, only half believing in any of it. Maybe if I'd kept that blue crystal and really learned how to use it, I'd be able to get myself out of this situation.

Now, I wanted to believe with everything in me, despite my lack of know-how. I squeezed the sea glass tighter. If I had any kind of magical abilities, now was the time to summon them.

Chapter Twenty-five

"KEVIN MARSHALL, KEEP YOUR hands where I can see them and turn around!"

My eyes sprang open. I had never been so happy to hear Aaron's voice.

But Kevin didn't immediately do what he was told. Then a few things happened at once. His eyes widened, looking crazed. And his hand with the knife came toward me.

"Noooo!" I tried with everything in me to roll out from under his foot, but he was still immovable. Something moved out of the corner of my eye, launching itself at Kevin's leg.

Kevin let out a long, pained cry and jerked to the side, missing me with his switchblade. I looked up to see Sherlock, still attached to Kevin's bare leg, just below the hem of his shorts. While Sherlock never used the full extent of his claws on me, I was well aware of how long and sharp they were. Now Kevin knew, too.

It took Aaron several long seconds to get across the rocky terrain to us, but thankfully it took Kevin even longer to get Sherlock off his leg, and as he struggled, I was able to get out from where he had me pinned.

I moved away as quickly as possible as Aaron moved in. "Kevin Marshall, you have the right to remain silent . . ."

Chapter Twenty-six

Aaron handcuffed Kevin and locked him in his police car before driving the three of us to the motel. He had already been in touch with Jay, and by the time we arrived, Jay had both of Kevin's parents already handcuffed and headed toward his own car.

Once he had them locked away, Jay, Aaron, and I all stood in a small circle between the two police cars in the motel's parking lot.

Aaron was the first to speak, extending a hand toward Jay. "Great job getting this one figured out, Jameson."

Jay smirked with one side of his mouth. "Great job saving Tabby."

Aaron dipped his head in a nod, and I blushed. I couldn't say why, but this unusual moment of praise between the detectives felt more like an understanding about me and their ongoing friendship with me than it had to do with the three people in the police cars who had conspired to commit murder.

There was a new sense of peace and camaraderie in the air, and I liked it. I liked it a lot.

It was a week later when I finally saw Jay again. Investigations—especially murder investigations—came with a lot of thorough questioning and paperwork. He dropped by my houseboat just as I walked out of the neighboring one, having checked it over before another renter was set to arrive. He met me on the dock near my boat and we both crossed the gangplank to sit on my front deck.

"So . . . are they all going to jail?" I wasn't sure what questions he was allowed to answer, but I couldn't seem to hold back the ones that had been plaguing me all week. I was especially glad that all my new witch friends had been found innocent in the investigation. "Did Kevin actually kill him? How were his parents involved?"

Sherlock lay in the sun a few feet away, feigning sleep, but I was certain he was hearing every word. Ever since my near-death experience, I'd been thinking a little differently about my cat. He was certainly more intuitive than any cat I'd ever met—not that I'd met a lot. Even though he'd helped save me on the beach, he'd also been the one to get me into trouble at the campground.

After a long week of pondering this, I had come to the conclusion that I could only blame myself. Sherlock had been given his blue crystals to wear by my aunt, likely with little choice over the matter. I had a choice, and so far I'd chosen to keep magic at a distance, even though it had proven to be helpful more than once. I was now convinced that if I'd spent time learning about the magical gift my aunt had once said I had, I would have been able to save myself out on that beach.

I was taking baby steps. I'd retrieved the blue crystal from the glove compartment of the boat, but so far, it had only made it as far as my aunt's kitchen table. Tonight, though, I planned to keep it beside my bed to see if it would bring on any mystical, magical dreams. I also planned to open up the conversation and learn from Rachael's experience, as flawed as it may be.

Jay went on to give me the case details, oblivious to my rabbit-trailing thoughts. "We've had to do a lot of back and forth interviewing to get to the truth. At first, Julie Marshall wouldn't stop confessing to murdering Bryan herself. But when we asked for specifics about where she killed him and how she moved his body and what time she'd left the houseboat, she didn't have good answers. She kept telling us that Kevin was innocent. That it was her and her husband's fault that

Kevin ever even had to meet Bryan Klaus."

"But she was only trying to save her son?" I guessed.

Jay nodded again. "Kevin overheard that his parents were planning a secret trip to Crystal Cove to repay Bryan Klaus for all he'd taken from their family. He heard his mom crying and saying she could never hurt anybody, no matter what he'd done to them, and his dad reprimanding her and telling her now was the time to be strong."

I couldn't seem to keep my mouth shut with all of my guessing. "So he was trying to save his mother and now she's trying to save him? They were all trying to save each other?"

Jay let out a humorless laugh. "Well, I don't think Jason Marshall was trying to save anyone's skin but his own. And the disappointing part is that he's the one behind all the rage of the situation. I don't think his wife or son would have thought of killing the man who had taken their business and humiliated them on their own. Kevin found the traveling carnival that would be stopping in Crystal Cove and got himself a job, determined to intervene before his mom did something she wouldn't be able to handle. By the time Jason and Julie realized where Kevin had gotten a job and that he was in Crystal Cove, it was too late. Kevin's plan to kill Bryan Klaus was already in motion."

"How did he do it all on his own?" I had just assumed Kevin and his dad had done it together.

"When he saw Klaus headed into the fun house to see why it was closed, Kevin sent Danny away from his post outside to get himself a hot dog. Danny didn't hesitate because Kevin said he'd watch the entry and besides, it would be closed for the rest of the night because of a mess some patrons had made inside. Kevin had planned to corner Klaus out behind the work trucks, but suddenly this seemed better and he raced to catch up to Klaus in the hall of mirrors. He killed him with the switchblade he carried and was just going to leave him in there to be found by the next set of patrons when he heard on his walkie-talkie that the Ferris wheel control was broken. He liked the idea of Klaus being discovered publicly much better and left with the large stuffed bear costume his dad had once had to wear on a wheeling cart containing the dead body. Later, when blood was found in the fun house, he suggested to Carl that he may want to get rid of Danny before the police found something on him."

I felt bad for the blue-haired carnie who had seemed nice enough and was innocent in all of this.

"I think his whole strategy to get away without being caught was to add as much confusion as possible."

Even though I knew Jay had been far from giving up on the case, I wondered how he ever would have gotten to the bottom of it if the carnival and the Marshalls had left town. I was thankful we had caught up with them in time.

"So now that this case is all tied up . . ." Jay looked at me with a smirk, and I wondered what was coming next. "I guess the only mystery is why you haven't invited me to accompany you to your school reunion yet?"

My face warmed. I had been trying not to think about my high school reunion, and trying even harder not to think of how much I'd like to go on a date with Jay. But it was getting more and more difficult now that the murder investigation was solved and I didn't have as much on my mind.

And perhaps it also had something to do with having the blue crystal close by.

He winked and added, "You know, just as friends."

I fingered the sea glass, hoping for some mental strength. I still didn't completely understand where its magical ability for me lay. It certainly hadn't given me any foreknowledge that this conversation was coming. "Well, I, um. Actually, I'm not going." This much was true. I'd decided that even though I was finding my own strength and place in this world, I wasn't ready to face up to high school bullies, even if they had matured. I certainly wasn't ready to face up to them and my dad on the same weekend.

He raised his eyebrows at me. "I thought you told your mom you would."

"The more I think about it, the more I feel like I don't want to go back to that back-biting high school crowd," I told him honestly. "Especially when I don't have much to show for my ten years out of high school."

He pulled back in surprise. "You? I'd think you'd be worried you might intimidate your classmates with all the experiences you've had since high school. Plus, you're a pretty amazing PI, and I'd tell that to anybody who asked."

I stared at him and imagined that scenario for a short moment. Walking around a Portland ballroom with Jay on my arm, having him tell all the back-biting girls I grew up with how awesome he thinks I am. It wasn't a bad thought. But it also wasn't the time.

Maybe I'd send some photos of the houseboat and Sherlock along to the reunion organizers. Maybe I wouldn't.

But my mom's loneliness was the bigger problem. As I thought of her and fingered my sea glass, a new thought came to me.

Maybe I was being selfish about keeping Crystal Cove to myself. Maybe I should invite her here. She had been Lizzie's half sister, after all. I'd been wanting to know more about my aunt, and if I ever planned to figure out how to successfully wield my own magic, maybe the key was getting to know my aunt better first.

As if Jay could read my mind, he sighed. "It's too bad. I hoped I was going to get a chance to meet your family."

"Well, you never know," I told him. My dad? Not on your life! But Mom and Pepper? I wasn't sure I was opposed to that idea.

"Just promise you'll think about it," he told me.

I nodded hesitantly, knowing my answer wouldn't change about my reunion. But Jay meeting my mom? Or Jay taking me out on a date sometime? Those I might consider.

And who was I kidding? With solving murders out of my mind and life back to normal, I likely wouldn't be able to think of anything else.

END OF BOOK 2

Join My Cozy Mystery Readers' Newsletter Today!

Would you like to be among the first to hear about new releases and sales, and receive special excerpts and behind-the-scene bonuses?

Sign up now to get your free copy of Mystery of the Holiday Hustle – A Mallory Beck Cozy Holiday Mystery.

You'll also get access to special bonuses to accompany this series—an exclusive bonus for newsletter subscribers. Sign up below and receive your free mystery:

https://www.subscribepage.com/mysteryreaders

Recipes: Enjoy Tabby's special coffee recipes from the summer fair!

Brown Sugar Irish Coffee

This recipe makes enough brown sugar syrup and whipped cream for several servings. Store the extra in the fridge until using.

Ingredients

1 cup dark brown sugar

1 cup water

1 cup heavy whipping cream

4 ounces freshly brewed hot coffee

1 ounce Irish whiskey or Irish whiskey flavored syrup

Instructions for the brown sugar syrup:

1. Place the brown sugar and water in a small saucepan and bring to a boil over medium-high heat.

2. Cook until the brown sugar dissolves.

3. Remove from heat and allow to cool to room temperature.

Instructions for the whipped cream:

1. Use a stand mixer with a whisk attachment or a hand-held whisk. Whisk the cream with 1/4 cup of the cooled brown sugar syrup until you lift the whisk and some of the thickened cream falls back in a ribbon and keeps its shape for a second or two.

Instructions for the Brown Sugar Irish Coffee:

1. Place the coffee and whiskey in an Irish coffee glass or coffee mug along with 1/2 ounce of the brown sugar syrup. (Use more or less according to taste.)

2. Top with plenty of the whipped cream and serve.

3. Add some coconut flakes to make Jay's special coffee.

<u>Coconut Iced Latte</u>
Ingredients:
2 cups espresso
2-3 cups unsweetened coconut milk
4 tbsp honey or maple syrup
1 tsp vanilla extract
a pinch of salt
Instructions:
1. Brew 2 cups of espresso.
2. Pour 1 cup of the espresso into an ice cube tray and freeze overnight.
3. Combine the hot espresso with the honey, sea salt, vanilla and coconut milk.
4. Adjust sweetness to your taste and refrigerate overnight.
5. Split the frozen espresso cubes between 2 mason jars. Add more plain ice cubes to fill the jars and pour the chilled latte over the top and finish with an extra splash of coconut milk.
6. Enjoy!

Frightful Friday

AN UPSET AT THE Harvest Festival , a Fright Night fundraiser with a deadly twist, and a realtor-turned-sleuth caught in the middle of both.

Tabby is finally ready to go on a casual fun date with Detective Jay Jameson at the local church's Harvest Festival, but her witch friends are holding their Fright Night fundraiser that same night. She feels caught in the middle of a long-standing quarrel between the two groups, especially when a dead body shows up at the center of it all.

As blame-shifting grows, will Tabby be able to figure out who is responsible for the corpse while keeping all of her friendships intact?

Order your copy of Frightful Friday now to find out!

Reviews Matter...

HONEST REVIEWS HELP BRING new books to the attention of other readers. If you enjoyed this book, I would be grateful if you would take five minutes to write a couple of sentences about it. You can find all the books in this series to leave reviews at the following link:

http://books2read.com/denisejaden

Thank you so much for your support. I couldn't do this without readers like you!

<u>THE TABITHA CHASE DAYS of the Week Mysteries</u>

- Book 1 - Witchy Wednesday

- Book 2 - Thrilling Thursday

- Book 3 - Frightful Friday
More titles coming soon!

<u>The Mallory Beck Cozy Culinary Capers:</u>

- Book 1 – Murder at Mile Marker 18

- Book 2 – Murder at the Church Picnic

- Book 3 – Murder at the Town Hall

- Christmas Novella – Mystery of the Holiday Hustle

- Book 4 – Murder in the Vineyard

- Book 5 – Murder in the Montrose Mansion

- Book 6 – Murder during the Antique Auction

- Book 7 – Murder in the Secret Cold Case

- Book 8 – Murder in New Orleans

Find all the Mallory Beck novels at bit.ly/MalloryBeck!

<u>Collaborative Works:</u>
- Murder on the Boardwalk
- Murder on Location
- Saving Heart & Home

<u>Nonfiction for Writers:</u>
- Writing with a Heavy Heart
- Story Sparks
- Fast Fiction

Denise Jaden is a co-author of the Rosa Reed Mystery Series by Lee Strauss, the author of several critically-acclaimed young adult and cozy mystery novels, as well as the author of nonfiction books for writers, including the NaNoWriMo-popular guide Fast Fiction. Her new Tabitha Chase Days of the Week Series will continue to launch throughout this year. In her spare time, she acts in TV and movies and dances with a Polynesian dance troupe. She lives just outside Vancouver, British Columbia, with her husband, son, and one very spoiled cat.

Sign up on Denise's website to receive bonus content as well as updates on her new Cozy Mystery Series.

www.denisejaden.com